THE BOVADIUM
FRAGMENTS

Works by J.R.R. Tolkien

THE HOBBIT
LEAF BY NIGGLE
ON FAIRY-STORIES
FARMER GILES OF HAM
THE HOMECOMING OF BEORHTNOTH
THE LORD OF THE RINGS
THE ADVENTURES OF TOM BOMBADIL
THE ROAD GOES EVER ON (WITH DONALD SWANN)
SMITH OF WOOTTON MAJOR

Works published posthumously

SIR GAWAIN AND THE GREEN KNIGHT, PEARL AND SIR ORFEO*
THE FATHER CHRISTMAS LETTERS
THE SILMARILLION*
PICTURES BY J.R.R. TOLKIEN*
UNFINISHED TALES*
THE LETTERS OF J.R.R. TOLKIEN*
FINN AND HENGEST
MR BLISS
THE MONSTERS AND THE CRITICS & OTHER ESSAYS*
ROVERANDOM
THE CHILDREN OF HÚRIN*
THE LEGEND OF SIGURD AND GUDRÚN*
THE FALL OF ARTHUR*
BEOWULF: A TRANSLATION AND COMMENTARY*
THE STORY OF KULLERVO
THE LAY OF AOTROU AND ITROUN
BEREN AND LÚTHIEN*
THE FALL OF GONDOLIN*
THE NATURE OF MIDDLE-EARTH
THE BATTLE OF MALDON
THE FALL OF NÚMENOR
THE COLLECTED POEMS OF J.R.R. TOLKIEN

The History of Middle-earth – by Christopher Tolkien

I   THE BOOK OF LOST TALES, PART ONE
II THE BOOK OF LOST TALES, PART TWO
III THE LAYS OF BELERIAND
IV THE SHAPING OF MIDDLE-EARTH
V   THE LOST ROAD AND OTHER WRITINGS
VI THE RETURN OF THE SHADOW
VII THE TREASON OF ISENGARD
VIII THE WAR OF THE RING
IX SAURON DEFEATED
X   MORGOTH'S RING
XI THE WAR OF THE JEWELS
XII THE PEOPLES OF MIDDLE-EARTH

* Edited by Christopher Tolkien

THE BOVADIUM FRAGMENTS

BY

J.R.R. Tolkien

Edited by
CHRISTOPHER TOLKIEN

Together with
The Origin of Bovadium
by
RICHARD OVENDEN

HarperCollins*Publishers*

HarperCollins*Publishers* Ltd
1 London Bridge Street
London SE1 9GF

HarperCollins*Publishers*
Macken House, 39/40 Mayor Street Upper
Dublin 1, D01 C9W8, Ireland

www.tolkien.co.uk
www.tolkienestate.com

Published by HarperCollins*Publishers* 2025

2

Text by J.R.R. Tolkien copyright © The Tolkien Trust 2025
Introduction, commentary and notes by Christopher Tolkien copyright
© the estate of C.R. Tolkien 2025
'The Origin of Bovadium' © Richard Ovenden OBE 2025
Illustrations by J.R.R. Tolkien copyright © The Tolkien Trust 1995, 2014,
2018, 2025

Publisher's note by Chris Smith © HarperCollins*Publishers* 2025

Photographs by Cas Oorthuys reproduced from *Term in Oxford*
(Bruno Cassirer (Publishers) Ltd, Oxford, 1963) figs. 8-11, 66,
84, 95, 96, 99, 116, 121-3, 127 & 140

Plans by Thomas Sharp reproduced from *Oxford Replanned*
(Architectural Press, Oxford, 1948)

☘®, 𝒥𝑅𝑅𝒯𝑜𝑙𝑘𝑖𝑒𝑛® and 'Tolkien'® are registered trademarks of
The Tolkien Estate Limited.

The Tolkien Trust and the estate of C.R. Tolkien have asserted their respective moral rights in this work. Richard Ovenden asserts the moral right to be identified as the author of 'The Origin of Bovadium' in this work.

The illustrations by J.R.R. Tolkien in this book are reproduced courtesy of the Bodleian Libraries, University of Oxford, from their holdings labelled MSS. Tolkien Drawings: 84, fol. 28r; 85, fol. 27; 86, fols. 15 & 20; 87, fols. 25 & 32; 88, fol. 22.

All manuscripts cited in 'The Origin of Bovadium' are held by
the Bodleian Libraries.

A catalogue record of this book is available from the British Library.

ISBN 978-0-00-873776-4

Printed and bound in Italy by Rotolito S.p.A.

All rights reserved. No part of this publication may be reproduced, stored in a retrieval system, or transmitted, in any form or by any means, electronic, mechanical, photocopying, recording or otherwise, without the prior permission of the publishers.

Without limiting the author's and publisher's exclusive rights, any unauthorised use of this publication to train generative artificial intelligence (AI) technologies is expressly prohibited. HarperCollins also exercise their rights under Article 4(3) of the Digital Single Market Directive 2019/790 and expressly reserve this publication from the text and data mining exception.

CONTENTS

Publisher's Note   vii
Introduction   xiii

THE BOVADIUM FRAGMENTS   1
Foreword   3
Fragment I   13
Fragment II   17
Fragment III   34
Postscript by the Editor   43
Other Texts of Fragment II   45

THE ORIGIN OF BOVADIUM   55

Acknowledgements   124

PUBLISHER'S NOTE

As Christopher Tolkien notes in his Introduction, *The Bovadium Fragments* was a 'satirical fantasy' written by his father. It grew out of a planning controversy that erupted in Oxford in the late 1940s when J.R.R. Tolkien was the Merton Professor of English Language and Literature.

Inspired by a comic poem, *Motor Bus* by A.D. Godley, of which he had received a copy, together with what he described as 'a recrudescence of the debate about Oxford roads', Professor Tolkien's tale was written initially for his own amusement, a private academic jest that poked gentle fun at such things as the 'pomposities of archaeologists' and 'hideousness of college crockery'. However, it was at the same time expressing a barbed *cri de coeur* against the inexorable rise of motor transport and 'machine-worship'

THE BOVADIUM FRAGMENTS

that was overwhelming the tranquillity of his beloved city. This was something of which Tolkien was acutely aware, as expressed in his letter to his son, Michael, written in 1952 when he and Edith were living in Holywell:

> 'We are having a very bad time here, as the traffic goes from mad to madder, and the past week-end was intolerable.' [*The Letters of J.R.R. Tolkien* (Revised and Expanded edition), #134a, p. 238]

The Tolkiens eventually escaped the din and disturbance and moved to 76 Sandfield Road in the spring of 1953, but the increasing volume of traffic was an ever-present cause of disruption for the city. Yet the solution proved to be less palatable than the cure. When writing to Michael Straight in 1956, Tolkien referred to the proposed 'Sharp plan' to provide a relief road through Christ Church Meadow:[1]

> '. . . the spirit of 'Isengard', if not of Mordor, is of course always cropping up. The present design of destroying Oxford in order to accommodate

---

1   See pp. 85 ff.

PUBLISHER'S NOTE

motor-cars is a case.' [*The Letters of J.R.R. Tolkien* (Revised and Expanded edition), #181, p. 340]

Christopher Tolkien remarks that, in the early 1960s, it seemed that *The Bovadium Fragments* might find its way to publication. By 1966, Tolkien's longtime publisher Rayner Unwin had given his endorsement of the work. Yet around this time, J.R.R. Tolkien also sought the opinion of Clyde Kilby, who was then assisting the professor with his preparation of *The Silmarillion*. Regrettably, Kilby demurred, concerned that the tragedy within the comedy might be disregarded, and the liberal use of Latin within the text might prove off-putting to modern readers; this lukewarm response was enough to persuade Tolkien to shelve it.

In this new edition, Christopher Tolkien has provided notes and commentary which serve to address Kilby's concern, and which will enable the reader to enjoy at last this tale of an imagined Oxford viewed through the lens of future (and not wholly reliable) academic study. As is now customary, his notes and commentary are printed in smaller type to that used for his father's text.

The tale is accompanied by a small selection of

THE BOVADIUM FRAGMENTS

illustrations by the author, some of them previously unpublished, which while not created specifically for this work, convey something of the tone and setting of the story, thereby enriching the tale. They may be found on pp. 1 ('London to Oxford through Berkshire'), 15 ('O to be in Oxford (North) now that Summer's here'), 20 ('Turl St., Oxford'), 26 (Untitled ['Alder by a Stream']), 29 ('Broad Street, Oxford'), 39 ('King's Norton from Bilberry Hill') & 44 ('The Wood at the World's End').[1]

In his essay, 'The Origin of Bovadium', which accompanies Tolkien's short story, Richard Ovenden OBE, Bodley's Librarian, paints a vivid portrait of Oxford during the first half of the twentieth century. The essay is illustrated with contemporary photos of the period by the award-winning Dutch photographer and designer, Cas Oorthuys, from his book, *Term in Oxford*, together with Thomas Sharp's actual plans that sparked the controversy. He also provides rich background to the *casus belli* which led to the furore that Tolkien witnessed first-hand, as the embers of debate between 'Town' (the municipal planners

---

[1] See *J.R.R. Tolkien: Artist & Illustrator* by Wayne G. Hammond & Christina Scull (figs. 7, 16, 19, 25 & 60) and *Tolkien: Maker of Middle-earth* by Catherine McIlwaine (fig. 63).

PUBLISHER'S NOTE

seeking to solve the city's notorious traffic congestion) and 'Gown' (the university colleges opposed to change) were fanned into flame.

Playful, erudite, and ultimately tragically moving, *The Bovadium Fragments* is like nothing else that J.R.R. Tolkien wrote, and its themes remain both provocative and timely. Within its lines may be found a concern for the fragility of our natural world, a love of which that was shared by both father and son. As Christopher Tolkien's final presentation of his father's work, it is therefore perhaps fitting that *The Bovadium Fragments* should be their coda.

CHRIS SMITH, 2025

INTRODUCTION

This work was certainly in being near the end of 1960: for on 25 October in that year my father's secretary, Elizabeth Lumsden, wrote to Rayner Unwin 'to ask on Tolkien's behalf the name of the current editor of the magazine *Time and Tide*. Tolkien wants to offer him a short piece he has written, "a sort of satirical fantasy"' (Christina Scull and Wayne G. Hammond, *The J.R.R. Tolkien Companion and Guide*, Vol. I, p. 593, citing Tolkien–George Allen & Unwin archive, HarperCollins). On the same day, Elizabeth Lumsden, in a letter in my possession, wrote to my father telling him that she had written to Rayner Unwin as requested, and also that she had 'typed half of the *Motores* MS and will finish it by the end of the week and send it to you'. On 28 October she wrote again (my father not being at home at that time) to say that Rayner Unwin knew the editor of *Time and*

THE BOVADIUM FRAGMENTS

Tide, and that my father was very welcome to use Rayner's name, if he wished, when submitting 'the Bovadium Fragments'; and she added: '*Please* try to ignore cold feet and just send it.'

Whether he did or did not do so I don't know; but some references bearing on the question of publication are given by Scull and Hammond, *op. cit.* pp. 707 and 774. In August 1966 Rayner Unwin wrote to him saying that he had read *The Bovadium Fragments* with pleasure and that he thought that my father should publish it in the *Oxford Magazine*; and in December 1968, in a letter to Rayner Unwin, he said of '*The End of Bovadium*' that he had 'no intention of publishing it now (if ever)'.

It is also recorded (*op. cit.* p. 707) that at some time in the summer of 1966 my father gave 'Bovadium' to Clyde Kilby to read, asking him if he thought it publishable. His comments, the only ones that I know of, survive, on a typescript slip preserved with the texts.[1] He told my father that he saw 'two difficulties'

---

1 Professor Clyde S. Kilby of Wheaton College, Illinois, stayed in Oxford from June to August 1966 to assist my father with *The Silmarillion*. An account of this is given in Scull and Hammond, Vol. I, pp. 701–2, who note that Kilby wrote comments on writings that my father gave him to read, and attached them to the manuscripts.

INTRODUCTION

(i.e. in the way of publication). One was that 'the use of Latin, clever as it is, becomes a stumbling block of an obvious kind for most people, even those of considerable education perhaps.' He had observed, presumably, that the Latin passages were translated, so that the mere presence of Latin would in his view constitute a stumbling-block. The second difficulty was the danger that readers wouldn't see 'the tragedy behind the comedy', for 'the motor has made itself so much a part of our lives' that any writing hostile to it would be simply disregarded. If these criticisms were accepted they would of course instantly sink the ship.

The initial inspiration for the work lay in verses entitled *Motor Bus* by A.D. Godley. From a letter found with the manuscripts and typescripts of *The Bovadium Fragments* it appears that my father received a copy of these verses from an acquaintance in April 1957. At the head of the printed page there is a cartoon sketch of a startled don in mortarboard and gown leaping, in the High Street at Oxford, out of the way of a 'double-decker' bus filled with men in bowler hats. The verses appear in two forms in *The Bovadium Fragments*, but in one case they are much changed, and in the other they are not precisely in the form as my father received them, which I print here.

THE BOVADIUM FRAGMENTS

MOTOR BUS

WHAT is this that roareth thus?
Can it be a Motor Bus?
Yes, the smell and hideous hum
Indicat Motorem Bum!
Implet in the Corn and High
Terror me Motoris Bi:
Bo Motori clamitabo
Ne Motore caeder a Bo –
Dative be or Ablative
So thou only let us live:
Whither shall thy victims flee?
Spare us, spare us, Motor Be!
Thus I sang; and still anigh
Came in hordes Motores Bi,
Et complebat omne forum
Copia Motorum Borum.
How shall wretches live like us
Cincti Bis Motoribus?
Domine, defende nos
Contra hos Motores Bos!

A.D. GODLEY, JANUARY 1914

INTRODUCTION

BUS STOP OUTSIDE QUEEN'S COLLEGE
ON THE HIGH STREET.

The poem was once widely known, and as presented here gives the impression of a page from an anthology. Alfred Godley (1856–1925) was a classical scholar at Oxford who became the Public Orator of the University.

My father sent me a copy of *The Bovadium Fragments*, I imagine about 1960, but his note which accompanied it has no date. His note reads:

THE BOVADIUM FRAGMENTS

The enclosed nonsense may afford you some passing amusement. It was produced by coming across the old verses of Godley together with a recrudescence of the debate about Oxford roads. But it has become overelaborated (from its original Fragment II) with elements of satire upon other things than 'machine-worship': the pomposities of archaeologists, the hideousness of college crockery, and what not. I am afraid the Latin portions are not very successful as imitations of the better sort of Dark Age or Biblical Latinity. Return at your leisure.

The comic point of Godley's verses lies in the absurdity, from an etymological point of view, of the word *bus*. It was a colloquial reduction of *omnibus*, which is the dative (also ablative) plural ending *-ibus* of the Latin word *omnis* 'all' (the ending is seen in *Motoribus* in line 18). This was derived from a French expression *voiture omnibus*, 'vehicle for all'. Godley treated the word *Bus* with the absurdity it deserved as if it were a noun of the Latin second declension, 'declining' like *Dominus* and a great many other words. Thus *Bum* in line 4 is the accusative or object case, like *Domin-um*. In 'Spare us, *Motor Be!*' (line 12) *Be* is the vocative case, the case of address to a person, as in the Latin

INTRODUCTION

line 19, *Domine!* '*O Lord!*' So also in lines 5–6, *Implet ... terror me Motoris Bi*, 'the terror of the Motor Bus fills me', where *Bi* is the genitive case of *Bus*; and in lines 7–8, *Bo Motori clamitabo ne Motore caeder a Bo*, 'I will cry out on the Motor Bus (dative case) lest I be slain by the Motor Bus' (ablative, this being the same as the dative in that declension). *Motores Bi* in line 14 is the nominative plural; *copia* ['abundance of'] *Motorum Borum* in line 16 the genitive plural; *cincti* ['encircled by'] *Bis Motoribus* in line 18 the ablative plural; and *Motores Bos* in the last line the accusative plural.

The word *motor* was derived from Latin, the radical meaning being 'that which imparts motion'. Godley declined this in his verses as a Latin noun, thus *Motorem* accusative in line 4, *Motoris* genitive in line 6, *Motori* dative in line 7, *Motore* ablative in line 8, *Motores* nominative plural in line 14, and accusative plural in line 20, *Motorum* genitive plural in line 16, *Motoribus* ablative plural in line 18.

There are as usual a number of pages of drafting in manuscript, but I will not go into this material in detail. It is sufficient to say that there is a complete manuscript which I will call 'M', roughly written but

THE BOVADIUM FRAGMENTS

legible, that contains the whole work, the opening discussions of the opinionated Doctors, the three 'Fragments', and the postscript by Dr Gums. In this text the unhappy city is named *Vadum Bovinum*, and the work as a whole *The End of Vadum Bovinum*.

Fairly closely following the texts in M are two typescripts, which can be called together 'T'. One of these was made by my father. The other is a carbon copy of this, but it extends only to Fragment I: from this point the text is a typescript made on a different machine by Elizabeth Lumsden, as mentioned on page xv (it may be that the remainder of the carbon copy was already lost).

It seems clear that 'T' was the 'final' text, and that this was what Rayner Unwin and Clive Kilby read in 1966.

In this edition I have only used the draft material to a very limited extent: chiefly a passage from a draft for Dr. Gums's piece that was rejected (pp. 11–12), and a poem with a Latin prose version that are given on pp. 46 ff.

CHRISTOPHER TOLKIEN

THE
BOVADIUM
FRAGMENTS

FOREWORD
by Doctor Sarevelk

Excavations have been proceeding for many years at *Vasti*, the prehistoric site in the midst of the marshes on the borders of the Southern Region. At first the results were disappointing. *Vasti* had evidently been evacuated after some catastrophe, and the area was for many centuries (how many it is not yet possible to calculate) completely abandoned, most of it reverting to wide swamps and dense thickets. But in the central site, a little raised above the marshes, a large population seems at one time to have been crowded for no discernible reason. Stranger still, it is now clear that this population was composed of two distinct peoples, speaking unrelated languages: A and B.

A was evidently the language of the primitive inhabitants, who long held out in the central and higher parts of the site, in what appears to have been a

THE BOVADIUM FRAGMENTS

number of irregular stone forts grouped on either side of a wide causeway climbing the eastward slope of a low eminence or 'academy'. B was the language of an incoming people from the North, of a somewhat higher cultural level. Before its disastrous end, however, the two peoples of *Vasti* had largely merged, and language B had almost entirely superseded A, even in the fortified central area.

The artefacts so far recovered present a confused picture. Most of them are indeed depressingly ugly and graceless. They evidently belong mainly to the A-people. Many fragments of clumsy and ill-made pottery in fact bear inscriptions or devices belonging to language A. Here and there, however, small hoards have been discovered, probably made at the time when the final catastrophe was approaching, in which a number of objects of very various cultural affinities are jumbled together. Some of these have artistic merit, and may be attributed to the speakers of language B.

Language B, for which much the most extensive material is available, has now been almost entirely deciphered and interpreted. The accomplishment of this task, long regarded as hopeless, is due to the labour of scholars working on the improbable, but in

FOREWORD

the result fruitful, guesses of Rotzopny and Dwarf, put forward 35 years ago. It was Rotzopny who first said: 'Let us assume that Language B, that of the higher culture, was actually related to our own, and see where that leads us.' It did not in fact lead anywhere, until Dwarf observed that the linear script used in formal epigraphy was evidently related to our own alphabet, but that the resemblance was greatly increased when it was noted that the Vastians had written everything backwards, so that words of language B must be held to a mirror in order to discover their connexion, if any, with those of our present tongue.

In this way the meaning of a number of basic words was soon established, and we may here neglect the debate that continues between those who hold that the Vastians actually spoke backwards, and those who assert that they merely wrote backwards, and being left-handed proceeded from left to right. Much more work was required before the relations between the different styles of writing were established. They are now roughly divided into types E, C, and F: the epigraphic, the cursive, and the so-called formal. C is careless, usually hideous and unskilled, and the relations of its letters to style E are largely obscured.

THE BOVADIUM FRAGMENTS

F provides one of the chief curiosities of Vastian culture. Few examples of this style have any beauty; but the professional scribes who used it achieved great skill, writing in regular compact hands of astonishing if somewhat lifeless uniformity.

In spite of this painstaking study our knowledge of language A remains very defective. It does not respond to the Rotzopny–Dwarf treatment, except in so far as its vocabulary contains a number of words similar to those of B, from which no doubt they were borrowed as the culture of the B-people became dominant. Until the discovery of the Fragments here published no useful bilingual texts had come to light. It was known that such things had existed, but the few specimens found were too brief and obscure to afford any assistance. Such texts were probably never produced in great numbers, since, naturally enough, the superior B-people would take little interest in the writings of the A-people; while the latter, as soon as they had begun to acquire the B-language, would abandon the archaic productions of their own primitive culture to the care of antiquarian scholars.

It will be at once perceived, therefore, that the 'Bovadium Fragments' have at least an exceptional linguistic interest. The interest of their contents is

FOREWORD

small; but as Dr. Gums points out, they offer two bilingual passages, one of considerable extent. These are still being studied.

SAREVELK.

* * *

These texts, the publication of which has been entrusted to me, as admittedly the chief expert in the Vastian language B, I have called the *Bovadium Fragments* for reasons which will be obvious to readers. Their order is determined by their contents. There are three fragments: F I, II, and III. F I appears to be the first leaf (all that has so far been found) of a chronicle or legend in language A. Of this F II is in my opinion clearly a translation, possibly somewhat expanded, into language B. Even in the present inadequate state of our knowledge of A it is evident that the opening part of F II closely agrees with F I; while it is notable that F II and F III present all names, as well as a number of other words, in forms belonging to language A. These are usually marked as alien elements by underscoring. Further, F III contains two chants, one in A and the other in B, while the context suggests that the second (in B) is a version or paraphrase of the former.

THE BOVADIUM FRAGMENTS

Dr. Sarevelk has spoken of the special interest that this has for linguistic scholars, and I will make only one further observation on this point. Even at the late period of F II and F III language A was not entirely forgotten, or no translation could have been made. That it was obsolescent, and known fully only to a few obstinate survivors of the A-people, is, however, revealed by the curious partial translation of the childish verses of the 'witty' Pius, which were clearly originally composed in A. This suggests that at the time of the production of F II, for the amusement, no doubt, of A-people, these now needed assistance in interpreting phrases in the 'elder tongue'.[1]

---

1 [GUMS.] *Elder tongue* and *popular*. These terms are taken from F III. It is true that the word here rendered *elder* is of uncertain meaning, and may be derived from language A: its written form is ИITAJ; but there can be no doubt that the description 'elder' is in any case appropriate. The term *popular* supplies further evidence that A, a primitive survival from a more barbaric time, was confined to the fortress or 'academy' of Vasti, while even the rustics of the surrounding country now spoke the more cultured language B, from which our own harmonious speech is ultimately derived. The alternative renderings, suggested to me by younger scholars, *native speech* or *vulgar tongue*, are thus clearly unsuitable. It may be noted that the hitherto unexplained word *academy, academia* is clearly shown by these texts to have referred to the inner fortress of Vasti. I have, however, retained it in my translation.

FOREWORD

Passages and words in this tongue have necessarily for the present been presented in a mere transcription. Language B, the 'popular',[1] has been translated; but your editor has taken the liberty of improving its rude and clumsy style and presenting a smooth and connected narrative, even at the risk of being criticized by some of the younger scholars for offering renditions that may in places appear bold and conjectural. Of the contents of these documents, dismissed somewhat hastily by my learned colleague, I will say no more, until readers have had the opportunity of perusing them.

GUMS.

THE BOVADIUM FRAGMENTS

Editorial note on the introductory remarks of Doctor Sarevelk and Doctor Gums.

The name *Bovadium*, bestowed on these fragments by Dr. Gums (and derived from the opening sentence of Fragment I) is found in the draft manuscript M (pp. xxi–xxii) in a fuller form, *Vadum Bovinum*, these being the Latin (i.e. 'Language A') noun meaning 'shallow water, ford' and the adjective *bovinus*, 'pertaining to oxen', thus the equivalent of Old English *Oxenaford* 'ford for oxen', modern *Oxford*.

The names of the learned Doctors will be found on inspection to conceal, by being written backwards, robust terms of disparagement in modern English. One other scholar of the Bovadium Fragments, a Dr. Sugob, is named, but his opinions do not appear in any text. The name *Vasti* is once found written *Vâsti*, indicating pronunciation of *Vâ* as in 'varlet', and the name is certainly to be explained as 'Varsity', a once frequent clipped form of 'University'. In draft texts the name was not *Vasti* but *Kadmi*, and this is clearly *Academy*, which Dr. Gums, in his footnote given above, interpreted as an unknown word referring to 'the inner fortress of Vasti'.

FOREWORD

A draft text of the foreword to the fragments, written by Dr. Gums, begins with material that my father subsequently dropped:

Investigation of the prehistoric remains in this island, begun barely a hundred years ago by a few adventurous enthusiasts, has only recently aroused general interest. Popular tradition, it is true, peopled the land 'once upon a time' with a race of giants who seem to have been busily employed in transporting large quantities of stone to inaccessible regions, and in excavating vast pits and tunnels for no ascertainable purpose. But the discovery fifty years ago of some fragmentary inscriptions roused the hope that some genuine information might at last be obtained, more interesting perhaps than such specimens of the artefacts, mostly hideous, as had so far been casually unearthed. Two difficulties delayed this hope. The centres of the 'lost culture', as it was somewhat rashly termed, were in remote regions, often in marshes, or in deep forests teeming with those intractable wild animals cats, and dogs. The rare inscriptions and written documents proved indecipherable. Courage and enthusiasm overcame, to some extent, the first obstacle. The second seemed hopeless. Even when

THE BOVADIUM FRAGMENTS

the expedition to *Kadmi* (which we know now to have been called Bovadium) discovered several inscriptions and a number of documents they remained useless. *Kadmi* as some may remember was selected partly because of almost superstitious awe in which the site was regarded in the country round.

Dr. Sarevelk's remarks on the 'formal' style of writing found in the Bovadium Fragments, that 'the professional scribes who used it achieved great skill, writing in regular compact hands of astonishing if somewhat lifeless uniformity', arose from his first acquaintance with typing and printing, as indicated by a pencilled note of my father's in the margin of one of the typescripts.

FRAGMENT I

[Note. The beginning of Fragment II is a rendering of this text into English.]

Urbs antiqua fuit Bovadium, ubi in aulis academiae vetustis multi studebant artibus, docti et discipuli. Via lata mediam urbem transibat, ex oriente in occidentem progrediens. Nihilominus diu tranquilla urbs manebat, et pace longa fruebantur incolae, laici et togati: horum sane nonnulli, ut ferunt, dormitabant in umbraculis suis. Olim autem nescioquis Daemonum secreta in officina machinas machinatus est nefarias, quibus nomen indidit Motores. Vulgus autem genus quoddam earum immane appellabat *Motorem Bum.*

Extemplo e latebris egressa haec monstra ingentia irruerunt in Bovadium et cum strepitu rotarum et magno ex intestinis foetore volvebantur per urbem; equos in fugam conjiciebant et pedestres venabantur

THE BOVADIUM FRAGMENTS

in viis. Tum vir quiddam facetiis inter academicos nobilis exclamavit in hunc modum:

> Unde venit fremitus?
> Numquid adest Motor Bus?
> Foetor fu! haud dubium
> Indicat Motorem Bum.
> Implet nunc in Cornethi
> Terror me Motoris Bi.
> Bo Mortori clamitabo,
> Ne Motore caeder a Bo.
> Heu fugaci victimae
> Parce, parce, Motor Be!

Mox autem, agminibus Motorum adeo multiplicatis ut titubarent aulae academicae, haec addidit:

> Dixerat. Innumeri
> Aderant Motores Bi.
> Iam complebat omne forum
> Copia Motorum Borum.
> Miseri qui vivimus
> Cincti Bis Motoribus!
> Domine defende nos
> Contra hos Motores Bos!

FRAGMENT I

Deus autem preces eius non exaudivit; at prolem maiorem continenter propagabant Motores, quia (turpe dictu) pars magna civium Bovadii his monstris hosp

[Here the fragment ends. It is written in a large irregular hand on both sides of a single leaf. Fragment II is in a second formal hand, small and astonishingly regular, written on one side only of five further leaves, found nearby but not attached to F I.]

* * *

THE BOVADIUM FRAGMENTS

Editorial note on Fragment I

In the original verses of Alfred Godley (p. xvi above) line 5 reads *Implet in the Corn and High*, these being colloquial shortenings of the names Cornmarket Street and High Street, which meet in a crossroads in the centre of Oxford. This is the form of the line as it appears in the text of the verses in Fragment II. These colloquialisms have been shortened further to the form in *Cornethi* (Corn et hi [high]) in the text in Fragment I.

Of Fragments I and II Doctor Gums remarked (see p. 7 above): 'F I appears to be the first leaf (all that has so far been found) of a chronicle or legend in language A. Of this F II is in my opinion clearly a translation, possibly somewhat expanded, into language B. Even in the present state of our knowledge of A it is evident that the opening part of F II closely agrees with F I. . . . That [language A] was obsolescent . . . is revealed by the curious partial translation of the childish verses of the "witty" Pius which were clearly composed originally in A.'

FRAGMENT II

There was an ancient city called *Bovadium*, where in the time-honoured halls of the academy many men, both learned and pupils, pursued the liberal Arts.

A wide street, the Via Maxima, crossed the city, being indeed of old a great highway by which men had travelled from the east to the western parts of the realm. Nonetheless the city was at this time quiet, and the inhabitants, both learned and lay, had long enjoyed peace; indeed it was said that in the academy many slumbered among their books.

But it came to pass that a *Daemon*[1] (as popular opinion supposed) in his secret workshops devised certain abominable machines, to which he gave the name *Motores*. Among them was a kind, especially huge, that became known to the vulgar by the inelegant title *Motor Bus*. One day, emerging suddenly from their hiding-places, these monsters rushed into

THE BOVADIUM FRAGMENTS

Bovadium, and with a din of wheels and great stench from their intestines they rolled through the city, putting horses to flight, and hunting pedestrians in the streets.

Hearing of this, one *Pius*,[2] well-known in the academy for his wit and skill in rhyme, composed these lines:

> What is this that roareth thus?
> Can it be a *Motor Bus*?
> Yes, the smell and hideous hum
> *Indicat Motorem Bum!*
> *Implet* in the Corn and High
> *Terror me Motoris Bi:*
> *Bo Motori clamitabo*
> *Ne Motore caeder a Bo* –
> Dative be or Ablative
> So thou only let us live:
> Whither shall thy victims flee?
> Spare us, spare us, *Motor Be!*

This rhyme, it is said, was chiefly intended as a jest for the amusement of his fellows, ridiculing the vulgar name of the monsters; for *Pius* himself had not as yet been troubled by them. But when, not

FRAGMENT II

long afterwards, the throngs of the *Motores* were so increased that the very halls of the academy were shaken, he added the further lines:

> Thus I sang; and still anigh
> Came in hordes Motores Bi,
> *Et complebat omne forum*
> *Copia Motorum Borum.*
> How shall wretches live like us
> *Cincti Bis Motoribus?*
> *Domine, defende nos*
> *Contra hos Motores Bos!*

The prayer of *Pius* was not answered. Indeed the *Motores* continued to bring forth an ever larger progeny; for (shame to relate) many of the citizens harboured the monsters, feeding them with the costly oils and essences which they required, and building houses for them in their gardens. For the *Daemon* promised to each separately that any *Motor* which he so tended would become his servant, and would bear him with great speed wherever he wished; and thus he would outstrip all other men, and he would, moreover, be rid for ever of the labour of walking. And to the *consiliarii*[3] of the city the *Daemon* said: 'Build now great pavilions for the *Motores Bi*, and behold! they will carry the citizens through the city, and into the city, and out of the city swiftly; and so any man will be able to dwell wherever he has a mind, even out in the beautiful country, and yet reach the place of his work more punctually than those who live in the narrow streets and walk like animals.'

FRAGMENT II

Soon, therefore, the stench of the *Motores* rose above the steeples of the city, and the din of their passing shook the halls and houses to their foundations. Men were rocked in their beds, but this did not induce sleep.

And daily the tumult increased, for the monsters had also been harboured in other towns, whose inhabitants rushed to *Bovadium*, or passed roaring through it, heedless of its inhabitants, or its academy, or even of its emporia.[4]

Then many citizens remembered the words of *Pius*, and they were no longer amused, saying openly that these *Motores* were ruining the city; but always they laid the chief blame on those who came from other towns. For most even of those who cried the loudest now had *Motores* of their own; and at that time the greatest anxiety of the citizens was still how to deal with them when they were not rolling on their wheels. Therefore they grudged the room taken up by strangers; for they themselves could no longer leave their own monsters idle in the squares and streets all day, until having finished drinking (or whatever other purpose had brought them into the town) they wished at last to roll home.

They began, therefore, to debate the 'Traffic

THE BOVADIUM FRAGMENTS

Problem', not meaning (as it appears) the making and selling of *Motores*, honourable occupations approved by the *Daemon*, but the performance by the monsters of the function for which they were constructed, rolling along roads. Many Planners then arose, who proposed this plan and that; but the only plan that was never put forward in any debate was that the *Motores* should be restricted or even prohibited. For at heart men were enamoured of the *Motores*; and the secret wish of every man was that he alone should possess a *Motor* and ride it at ease, but other men should go on foot and preserve the peace. Indeed at that time (while *Motores* could still move about the country) men were for ever riding here and there looking for peace, which their *Motores* destroyed as soon as they found it. Any man who could not afford a *Motor* of his own in which he could go in search of peace, envied those who could; and some sold their children into slavery, or anything else they could spare, and offered gold to the *Daemon*, if he would provide them with *Motores* faster than those owned by their neighbours, so that they could find peace before their neighbours got there. And since the *Motores* proved to be as short-lived as they were voracious, and those who had once kept one wished

FRAGMENT II

always for a successor, nothing came of the debates; for no one would listen to any plan that might hinder the supply of new monsters.

Therefore, highly pleased, the *Daemon* saw to it that his agents produced more and more *Motores*; and he laughed, for no one seemed yet to have perceived the fraud that he had practised. He had promised speed; and he had promised ease and the saving of time. But as for speed: before long the *Via Maxima* was packed with an unceasing stream of *Motores* crawling so slowly from halt to halt that a man on foot could (like an animal) walk its whole length and back to find a 'mounted' friend only ten yards further on his way, while the horn of his *Motor* trumpeted in vexation. And as for ease: the 'owners' now had a multitude of cares (tending the ailments of the monsters, and seeking places where to leave them) which consumed most of their time to no purpose.

It is true that there were not a few who had ceased to govern their *Motores*, but had become their servants, finding their chief pleasure in waiting on them. Such men cared very little what their *Motores* did, so long as their skins shone and they purred. Indeed on the days formerly set aside for prayers and rites in the temples many would now wheel their *Motores* out upon a platform before their houses and there tend them and worship them, prostrate upon the ground. On these days the *Motores* looked indeed as if prepared for a great ceremony, but their 'owners' were content with the dirty garments of slaves.

There remained, however, many, not yet so besotted, who in their innocence expected the *Motores* to earn their keep; and they were disappointed. For they discovered that if they proposed to 'go by *Motor*', they might indeed (when fortunate) 'go', but they could do nothing else: on the way they could neither think nor speak nor look aside; and when (if still more fortunate) they arrived they were exhausted; for they were consumed by anxiety, either to avoid being trapped immovably in a press of other *Motores*, or if they found a freer road to escape violent death. For those who had purchased 'speed' now often sat for hours looking at the unsavoury hinder-end of a *Motor* in front, and so great a fury was engendered in them that, when released, they rushed headlong like madmen, slaying any fools on foot that they met, or crashing recklessly into rival *Motores*. In this way thousands were dismembered or burned to death.

Nevertheless the constipation of the highways did not mitigate the noise and stench in the city; for

FRAGMENT II

if halted the *Motores* belched the more, while they drummed and throbbed inwardly in thwarted rage. No longer could any man converse with another in the streets save in hoarse shouts and at the peril of choking in poisonous fumes. Behind padded doors and doubled windows the *consiliarii* and *magistri* of *Bovadium* lifted up their voices in lamentation and laid their aching heads together; and the Planners brought plans to them. But the only remedy that they had devised was the making of still more roads (for the use of the *Motores*) by the destruction of ancient buildings, the devastation of fields, and the felling of trees. This all agreed was wise; but on the placing of the roads there was no agreement. For each Planner was most disposed to the destruction of houses, fields and groves that belonged to other men, who could be robbed and ejected 'for the common good'; and the most plansome were naturally those who possessed none of these things, or had no love for them, since their fame and livelihood depended upon their removal.

Now it came to pass that for the assistance of the *consiliarii* and *magistri* many maps of *Bovadium* were made; and thus those who lived upon the northern side of the *Via Maxima* (where the din and stench was worst) became aware that those who lived upon its southern side were secretly enjoying a remnant of the peace of old. For their halls looked southward over meadows and groves through which in former days no road had ever been made, and into which, the approaches being guarded by great gates and iron bars, no *Motor* could enter (save a few belonging to southern magnates). Then the Northerners were filled with hate and envy, holding the opinion that misery should be equal, or if unequal that other men should bear the heavier burden; and their hatred was in no way appeased when the Southerners pointed out that

FRAGMENT II

all citizens were free to enter their meadows and there escape for a while the pursuit of the *Motores*; for the Northerners begrudged to the Southerners the view from their back-windows.

Therefore the Northerners laid the matter before the Minister, who was a man appointed by the King to deal (if he could) with the troubles caused by the *Motores*; and he had great powers to command the destruction of any land or property, as he saw fit, if thereby the *Motores* were enabled to continue rolling. This man the Northerners now besought to order the building of a great road and bridges through the southern meadows, so that the *Motores*, deserting the *Via Maxima*, might transfer their din and stench to their neighbours, but they themselves might sleep in peace.

The Southerners, however, preferred their own good fortune to the 'common good' (or common misery), and filled in their turn with rage they contested this plan with great bitterness. But while this new debate was proceeding, still the *Motores* increased in size and numbers. Fearing, therefore, that the Minister might yield to the clamour of their enemies (if only to appear to the King an active man, worthy of the very large *Motor* that had been given to him), the

THE BOVADIUM FRAGMENTS

Southerners determined to distract him with other proposals. They therefore brought to his notice plans more attractive, pointing out the obvious advantages of making new roads and bridges in northern territory, or at least in places neither visible nor audible from southern windows. That even larger numbers of habitable houses and fruitful fields would in these ways be destroyed was held to the credit of the plans; for it was well known that Ministers did not count costs (incurred by other people), and favoured plans that were 'bold': a term that at that time was applied to any action that hurt someone else.

The Minister, however, took no action one way or the other. The arguments on either side appeared to him equal; and he was in fact in possession of plans even bolder, which would have effectually ruined both the south and the north simultaneously. No doubt he found these attractive. The academy in *Bovadium* was ancient, beautiful, and even moderately useful, and the damage would, or course, be irreparable; so that if a man ordered it, no one could possibly doubt that he was active, serious, and indeed endowed with 'vision'. He was, however, engaged with more urgent matters.

* * *

FRAGMENT II

Though in *Bovadium* this was usually forgotten, similar troubles had arisen in every part of the realm. Many other cities were even more grievously afflicted; while the Capital City itself had become an almost solid mass of *Motores*. The Minister had accordingly long been occupied – at vast cost and by turning many thousands of acres into permanent desert – in constructing great roads, on which the more expensive

THE BOVADIUM FRAGMENTS

kinds of *Motores* (such as his own) might be able to proceed at full speed. Nonetheless he was unable to reach *Bovadium*. The new roads at once became blocked with streams of competing *Motores*, and by those that were derelict at the road-side, overcome by their frantic exertions. In this case the Minister found himself, and after spending a cold night in his *Motor* he returned, at great hazard, to the Capital City, from which he was not again able to escape.

Therefore day by day the uproar and stench went on increasing in *Bovadium*, until the voices of the debaters and the lamentation of the afflicted, and even the shouts of the Planners, could be heard no more. And so the matter ended. There came at last a day when every street, every road, lane, alley, court, and byway was blocked: nothing could move either forward or backward. All *Motores* stopped dead. Silence fell. The silence of a tomb. For when at length men came to the city, walking over the tops of the inert *Motores*, they found that all the inhabitants were dead. Slain by the poisonous fumes, their shades had fled to seek a cleaner air in Hell.

There now (it is said) they stood, deaf ghosts, upon the shores of *Styx*;[5] and they saw to their dismay that they were only part of a great host.

FRAGMENT II

They began to murmur; but a large Shade stood forth and ordered them to form themselves into lines: and they saw that this was the Minister.

'You can rely on me,' he said. '*Charon*[6] has been removed for inefficiency. By arrangement with the *Daemon* a fleet of *cymbae motrices*[7] has been prepared. I regret that the fare has been raised to six obols.[8] Please have them ready. Keep your places. There is no longer any hurry, and there is plenty of room for all, on the other Side.'

No ghost paid any attention to him.

* * *

THE BOVADIUM FRAGMENTS

Editorial notes on Fragment II

1. The spelling *Daemon* represents the Greek and Latin form of the word from which demon is derived, and was often used in English to indicate the ancient meaning, an attendant or indwelling spirit, a guardian god that guides a man in his life. It may be thought that this was my father's intention. See further the reference to the *Daemon* in Fragment III.
2. *Pius* represents the name *Godley*.
3. *consiliarii*: 'counsellors, advisers'.
4. *emporia*: The word emporium was derived from Greek *emporion*, Latin *emporium*, meaning a place of commerce, a market. My father sometimes used it, in mild derision, of very large department stores, and that is no doubt the force of the word *even* here.
5. *Styx*: In Greek mythology, the chief river of Hades, the underworld, the realm of the dead.
6. *Charon* was the ferryman who carried in his boat the shades of the dead across the river Styx to Hades.
7. *cymbae motrices*: 'motor boats'. My father clearly used the rare word *cymba* (also *cumba*) here because it was specially associated with Charon's boat, as in Virgil, *Aeneid* VI.303.

FRAGMENT II

8 *six obols*: Charon received a fee of one *obol* for each ghostly passenger; and for payment of this fare the dead were buried with a coin of this value in their mouths.

FRAGMENT III

[Note. Dr. Gums remarked (p. 7): 'F III contains two chants, one in A and the other in B, while the context suggests that the second (in B) is a version or paraphrase of the former.']

[Here on three further attached pages a third somewhat larger but equally regular hand adds the following legend.]

It is said that in that time an old man stood and gazed at the desolation about him; and after a while he lifted up his voice in a chant, made in the elder tongue and after the manner of the chants that in former days had been heard in the temples of *Bovadium*; and it purports to relate the answer given to the cry of the *magistri*: *Domine defende nos*. Thus he sang:

FRAGMENT III

Dixit Dominus dominis et magistris: 'Quare tristes estis, et quare conturbatis aurem meam?
Nonne locuti estis in vanitate: velociores ventis erimus; quaecumque volumus faciemus illico?
Ecce, pedes habetis et non ambulatis; titubatis in cluribus vestris.
Stridore rotarum vehimini; motiones vestras sine consilio.
Pax deseruit hortos vestros, et quies dereliquit cubilia.
Deus vester facta est Machina quam machinamini ipsi; idola eius multiplicata sunt nimis.
Ferrum in cordibus eorum; in ventribus comprimuntur ignes.
Foetor procedit e visceribus; cornua eorum spargunt fremitum.
Similes iis fient qui faciunt ea, et omnes qui diligunt illa.
Servient operibus manuum suarum, in omnibus diebus suis servi.
Aures habent et fient surdi; nares habent et non odorabuntur.
Oculos habent at videbunt mortem: cadavera in viis bituminatis.
In vanum fugient pestem quam meditati sunt; ipsa deducet eos in infernum.'

THE BOVADIUM FRAGMENTS

Sed nos qui vivimus laudabimus opera Domini nostri: Deus vivus omnia viventia fecit.
Domine, a machinis defende nos, qui dileximus terram quam tu fecisti.[1]

Thereupon a number of the 'rescuers', being mostly country-folk who had crept into *Bovadium* to see what they could see and find what they could find, drew near, attracted by the strange singing. Seeing them the old man took off his hat, and began to chant again in the popular speech; for the bystanders did not look the sort of men to understand the elder tongue; and the members of the Academy were now on the far side of *Styx*. Thus he sang again:

'The Lord said unto the doctors and masters: "Why are ye sad, and why do ye trouble my ear? Did you not speak in your folly, saying: we shall be swifter than the winds; whatsoever we wish we shall do straightway? Lo! ye have feet and ye walk not; ye totter upon your legs. With a great din of wheels ye are borne about; your motions are without purpose. Peace hath deserted your groves, and rest hath forsaken your couches. Your god ye have made a Contrivance which ye yourselves contrived;

FRAGMENT III

its likenesses are multiplied exceedingly. Iron is in their hearts, and in their bellies fires are imprisoned. Stench proceedeth from their entrails; their horns cast abroad a great noise. Like unto them shall become those who make them, and all those who hold them in esteem. They shall serve the works of their own hands, slaves in all the days of their life. They have ears, and they shall be made deaf; they have nostrils, and they shall perceive no odour. Their eyes shall see only death: the corpses on the roads of pitch. In vain shall they flee from the plague which they have devised; it shall bring them down upon the way to Hell.'"

At that point many of those that stood by became angry, crying out that the singer was mad, or that he blasphemed; and some said to him: 'Why do you not mention the *Daemon*? And why do you attribute to men the devising of the *Motores*, which were His? He will be ill pleased if He hears you. As well He may. For is not one of his great places nearby, even in *Vaccipratum*,[2] as we have been told?'

But the singer looked at them with pity, saying: 'Nay, he will not be displeased; for this work of his is finished to his liking. And as for *Vaccipratum*, and other places like it, he did not dwell there. Men worked there, to make the things that you clamoured for. Now they are buried under piles of *Motores*, made and half-made, which no man can move. There they will rot; for the *Daemon* is no longer interested in them. His *phrontisterium*[3] is elsewhere, and that workshop at least is not yet closed; its products are easily transported. No doubt it will produce some new Plan to persuade you to use your skill in some other lunatic fashion – one day. But be of good cheer! It may be a long time before your children's children hear of it. You yourselves will be too hungry, scraping your living (like animals) among the ruins, to give thought to such follies. Go and look for some food!'

Then the bystanders scratched their heads. His last remark was the only one that they understood. Some, therefore, went to look for food; but a few of the more foolish went to look for *Motores* of the better sort, hoping to get them out of the deadlock, for many of the monsters still had fuel in their bellies. But some could not be roused again, and the others, though they spluttered and roared, could not move a foot in any direction. Whereupon one of the men in a rage cast a lighted match into the belly of one of

FRAGMENT III

the monsters; and there was a sudden thunder and a great blaze, in which he and his fellows perished. For the fool had thrown his match into a *Motor* that had been bearing a huge load of fuel for the feeding of other *Motores*. Then the fire leaped from belly to belly among the monsters, until throughout the city there was a great burning. So ended *Bovadium*.

Later it came to pass even as the singer had said. There was a great dearth of food: because of the devastation of fertile lands by roads and by the excavation of materials for roads. There were no horses left to help men; and for the *Motores* that had driven them out there was no fuel, and no slaves to tend them. So that such lands as remained were poorly tilled, or not at all. Thus to dearth succeeded famine, in which most of those who remained alive in the beautiful

THE BOVADIUM FRAGMENTS

country finally perished. Then most of the survivors fled into the wilds far from the roads and shunned the sight of the *Motores*, which were hideous in decay. But here and there the rude villagers used them for the housing of their starveling fowls; and so at last they produced something for the common good, for the hens on their seats laid a few eggs: small, but at any rate fresh.

* * *

Editorial notes on Fragment III

1 The last two sentences of the Latin text are not translated into the 'popular speech'. They read in English: 'But we who live will praise the works of our Lord: the living God made all living things. Lord, from these devices deliver us, who have loved the earth which thou hast made.'

2 *Vaccipratum*: 'Cow-pasture' (Latin *vacca* 'cow', *pratum* 'meadow'), a name devised by my father to represent the English name *Cowley*, which he derived from Old English *Cū-lēah* of the same meaning. Later he pencilled this note on the typescript: '*Vacciprata* was, curiously, the actual name of some gardens in Rome.' Cowley was the village to the south of old Oxford where William Morris (Viscount Nuffield) went to school and where he built his huge motor-car factories.

3 *phrontisterium*: This arcane word carries a memory of Athens in the fifth century B.C., when there appeared the play *The Clouds* by Aristophanes. This was an attack on Socrates and his school, which was ridiculed as the φροντιστήριον, a 'thinking-shop' (the usual translation). Behind this name are the words

THE BOVADIUM FRAGMENTS

φροντίς 'thought', 'meditation', φροντίζω 'to think; think out, devise', and φροντιστής 'a deep thinker', as Aristophanes derisively called Socrates. For the occurrence of *phrontisterion* (or Latinised *phrontisterium*) in English see the Oxford English Dictionary, entry *Phrontistery*.

POSTSCRIPT
BY THE EDITOR

I feel confident that those who have read these curious documents will have discovered in them more than a mere linguistic interest. They throw a considerable light on the 'lost culture'. How far they can be regarded as historical is another matter. Although several of the younger school have already assumed that *Bovadium* was the ancient A-name of *Vasti*, the assumption is rash. When the A 'chronicle' was written *Vasti* must have been still flourishing. *Bovadium* must, therefore, refer to some other place, most probably to a place and time that never existed outside the morbid fancy of some late writer among the decadent A-people. His tale is quite incredible. It is hard to believe that there were ever in this country so many men or so rich. It is impossible to believe that, if so, they would squander all that they had in such a 'lunatic fashion'.

THE BOVADIUM FRAGMENTS

We at any rate are not likely to fall into such folly. We do not believe in any *Daemon*; and if we did, we should give no ear to one that prompted us to the making of large machines. For happily we value peace, and food, and the visual arts; and the science to which we are most devoted is Medecine, somatic and psychic. At present, indeed, as we all know, we are on the brink of great advances; and the hope is now near that we shall at last conquer mortality, and not 'die like animals': to quote the words of our leading Thanatologist. Some think that he is inspired.

GUMS.

OTHER TEXTS OF FRAGMENT II

The two texts that follow, a poem in octosyllabic couplets and a passage of Latin prose, are very closely related in narrative content. Both are written in a good clear hand, and may well have been composed at the same time: the Latin prose, I would suggest, being based on the poem.

It will be seen that both texts take up at the point where, after the last lines of the 'Motor Bus' poem, which are cited in both, Fragment I has 'Deus autem preces eius non exaudivit' (p. 15) and Fragment II 'The prayer of Pius was not answered' (p. 19); but then they move almost at once to the estrangement and hostility of those that dwelt to the north and to the south of the Via Maxima, to the total paralysis of the city, and the gathering of the dead 'motorists' on the shores of the Styx.

THE BOVADIUM FRAGMENTS

At the end, where in Fragment II (p. 31) the 'Shade of the Minister' informed them that Charon had been dismissed and that 'by arrangement with the *Daemon* a fleet of *cymbae motrices* has been prepared' to ferry them across the dismal river, in the present texts Charon, still present, beckons them to his Motor-boat: and in the text of M (see pp. xxi–xxii) the same is told: 'There now (it is said) they stood, deaf ghosts, upon the shores of Styx, and saw to their dismay grim Charon beckoning them – to his "motor-boat".'

There seems to be no trace in the draft material of how my father may have intended this poem and its Latin prose companion to stand in relation to the existing *Bovadium Fragments*.

There follows here, first, the poem, in thirty-one octosyllabic couplets.

Domine defende nos contra hos Motores bos!
A.D. Godley, 1914

Alas! that prayer was never heard:
Jove's ears, maybe, were rendered surd;
for Motors prolific bred and teemed;

OTHER TEXTS OF FRAGMENT II

from near and far to Town they streamed,
hunting their prey with hooting shrill
from Iffley turn to Hinksey Hill.[1]
Their stink above the steeples went;
stones were shaken and ears were rent
by din of wheels and engine-blare.

And in those days no man would dare
on foot to cross the reeking High,
unless he suddenly would die;
and thus the North-folk and the South
conversed no more by word of mouth;
the town divided, tongues were changed,
and sundered men became estranged.

The North folk then became aware
that Motors by a fraud unfair
their Southern neighbours did not vex
with bang and blast of Shell and Mex;
for these had never suffered road
of tar to pass their quiet abodes.

Against the South in envious hate

---

1 *from Iffley turn to Hinksey Hill.* – Hinksey Hill rises between the villages of North and South Hinksey to the south-west of Oxford, and Iffley lies to the south-east on the other side of the Thames, not far from Cowley (see the note on *Vaccipratum*, p. 41).

THE BOVADIUM FRAGMENTS

the North then sent a delegate,
and begged the King to build a street
and bridges through the meadows sweet
of Southern folk, that Motors might
desert the High and bring their blight
of stench and din among the trees,
but they themselves should sleep at ease.
    Then red with wrath the South arose
to battle with their Northern foes
yet neither side, though hot with hate,
could crush the other in debate.
So then the Southern folk took thought,
and in their turn the King besought
rather to break the North-men's halls,
blow up their houses, mine their walls,
that so might in unhindered flow
yet more and swifter Motors go
slap through the Town, but peace of old
should still the southern meads enfold.

    The King did nothing. Yet each day
louder and larger the array
of Motors grew, until no more

OTHER TEXTS OF FRAGMENT II

the voices of that wordy war
were heard beneath the savage roars
of huge mechanic carnivores.
    Thus came the end of battle long:
so deep and dense became the throng
of Motor-cars that every street,
byway, and lane was choked, replete
till blocked in endless lines at last
immovable no Motors passed.
All stopped. And then a silence fell:
the silence of a tomb. To Hell
to seek a cleaner air long forth
had fled the souls of South and North.
Slain by the all-pervading stink,
deaf ghosts they stood on Styx's brink,
aghast to see fell Charon gloat,
beckoning them to his Motor-boat.

There follows now the second of these texts, in Latin prose; at the end of it I have added a translation.

Domine defende nos contra hos Motores bos!

THE BOVADIUM FRAGMENTS

Sed Dominus [> Deus] preces eius non exaudivit; at prolem propagabant innumerabilem Motores Bi, usque donec fere cives et togati[1] vehebantur Motoribus, et ascendebat putor in fastigias ædium, et cælum concutiebat fragor.

Et in diebus illis nemo audebat pedester transire Viam Maximam propter periculum mortis; et divisa est urbs, et quia non loqui poterant Australes cum Septentrionalibus, diversae factæ sunt linguæ eorum, et alienati sunt.

Tum videntes Motores non vexare Australes (quod hi nullam viam pica tam agros suos transire siverant) magnum odium Australium ceperunt Septentrionales; et orabant Cæsarem viam struere et pontes per australia prata, ut Motores relicta Via Maxima transferrent putorem suum and fremitum in lucos et hortos Australium, sed ipsi viam habitarent quietam.

Tunc ira magna affecti surgebant Australes in

---

1 The phrase *laici et togati* is used in Fragment I (p. 13), and the words used in the corresponding place in Fragment II (p. 17) are 'both learned and lay'. The adjective *togatus* means 'wearing a *toga*' (the cloak-like outer garment of a Roman citizen), but my father was using the word in a transferred sense, a robe of office; in *laici et togati* 'learned and lay' he was clearly thinking of the gowns of the scholars of the 'academy' of Vasti.

I suppose the same is true of *cives et togati*, but – in the spirit of Dr. Gums, p. 11 – I have left 'wearers of the toga' in my translation.

OTHER TEXTS OF FRAGMENT II

Septentrionales, et proeliis factis neutri superabant. Australes igitur Cæsarem appellabant vicissim, perfodere potius redificia Septentrionalium, ut Motores crebrius and velocius possent percurrere urbem, et antiqua maneret quies australis.

Sed Cæsar neutrum fecit. At multiplicatis indies Motoribus, adeo increscebat fragor ut voces altercantium nemo diutius audire possset. Ita finita est causa: tot et tanti facti sunt Motores ut omnes vias et calles obstruxerunt; et densis tandem constipatis agminibus ipsi immobiles conticuerunt omnes; tum demum silentium. Silentium autem sepulcri. Jamdudum et Australes et Septentrionales ex putore erant mortui. Puriorem in infernis aerem petentes umbræ surdæ steterunt denique Stygis in ripa, attonitæ et deiectæ. Atrox ibi indicavit iis Charon cymbam sua motricem.

But the Lord [> God] did not hear his prayers; the Motores Bi brought forth a countless progeny, until almost all the citizens and wearers of the toga were borne in Motors, and the stench rose up to the tops of the buildings and the noise shook heaven.

And in those days no one on foot dared to cross the Via Maxima on account of the danger of death; the

THE BOVADIUM FRAGMENTS

city was divided, and since the Southerners could not speak with the Northerners their languages became divided, and were estranged.

Then, seeing that the Motors did not harass the Southerners (because they allowed no tarred road to cross their fields) the Northerners were seized by a great hatred of the Southerners; and they entreated the King to build a road and bridges across the southern meadows, so that the Via Maxima being deserted the Motors would transfer their stink and roaring to the groves and gardens of the Southerners, but they themselves still dwelt in quiet.

Then in great rage the Southerners arose against the Northerners, but in their battles neither overcame the other. The Southerners therefore in their turn called upon the King to dig up rather the buildings of the Northerners, so that Motors in greater numbers and more speedily could dash through the city, and the ancient southern quiet would endure.

But the King did neither. Yet with the Motors multiplying every day the noise increased so greatly that no one could any longer hear the voices of the disputants. And thus the matter came to an end: so many Motors were made that they blocked up all the streets and alleys; and at length, in densely packed

OTHER TEXTS OF FRAGMENT II

lines immovable all fell still, and then silence. But the silence of the grave. Both Northerners and Southerners were long since dead of the fumes. Seeking a purer air in Hell they stood at last, deaf ghosts, on the bank of Styx, awestruck and cast down. There fierce Charon pointed out to them his Motor-boat.

THE ORIGIN OF
BOVADIUM

THE ORIGIN OF BOVADIUM

J.R.R. Tolkien arrived in Oxford in the autumn of 1911 to begin his first year as an undergraduate at Exeter College. Until his death more than sixty years later the city and the University would be a central point in his existence, the main context in which his scholarly, creative, social and family lives would operate. At the time he arrived in Oxford a very modern mode of transport – the motor car – was beginning its journey to become the dominant industry in the city, one that would have massive influence on both its urban and its social landscape. The University had been at the heart of Oxford, evolving the way the city looked and operated over many centuries, but the motor industry would make its mark much faster. The collision between Tolkien's life as a scholar and writer in the ancient University, and the impact of modernity through the increasing use of the motor car, would eventually lead Tolkien to write *The Bovadium Fragments*, a satirical tale set long in the future that neatly combined Tolkien's life as a scholar working on manuscripts, with his incredulity that mankind should become so intensely obsessed with the automobile (and all that came with it).

The Dwelling of the Genius of Repose

The Oxford that welcomed Tolkien in 1911 was still essentially a small market town, the centre of a mainly rural community, but one with a celebrated University, the oldest in the English-speaking world, and one that ranked in reputation as one of the greatest seats of higher learning. Viewed from a raised vantage point such as the roof of the Radcliffe Camera (access to which could be had for a small sum), the boundaries of the city could be easily seen – the surrounding wooded hills of Cumnor, Wytham and Shotover clearly visible in the distance. Even Headington, now very much a suburb of Oxford, was at that time still officially a village in the county and not administratively part of the city. The historic heart of Oxford was already a tourist destination, and had been for

THE ORIGIN OF BOVADIUM

OXFORD'S DREAMING SPIRES

some considerable time. The colleges had occupied the same locations, in a complex pattern of small streets through a process of gradual development and expansion which had begun in the thirteenth century. Medieval buildings predominated but there were handsome stone structures of later periods which added to the richness of the urban landscape, many of them designed by the nation's most famous architects: Christopher Wren's Sheldonian Theatre, Vanbrugh's

Queen's College, Hawksmoor's Clarendon Building are just a few examples. The Victorian era added some much newer architectural elements to many of the colleges, and some University institutions, such as the University Museum, as well, but they were for the most part designed in the predominant Gothic revival style of the late nineteenth century, and as such blended almost seamlessly in with the genuine Gothic of the older colleges.

The central parts of Oxford were, however, not purely the domain of the University. Small shops and private housing could be found dotted in the streets among the colleges, with the city's main shopping streets of Queen Street, Cornmarket and George Street being only a few steps away from University buildings. Markets were still a major part of the city's life for buying and selling fresh food, most of it produced locally. The central part of the city is bisected still by the imposing, wide High Street, known as 'The High'. The High was one of the grandest streets in Britain outside the major cities. Running from Magdalen Bridge at its eastern end up to Carfax, the public water conduit at the heart of the city where four roads meet from the city's four ancient gates, the High had a pleasing mixture of imposing stone

THE ORIGIN OF BOVADIUM

TRAFFIC UNDER THE BRIDGE OF SIGHS
(HERTFORD COLLEGE)

THE BOVADIUM FRAGMENTS

buildings of ancient colleges (such as Magdalen, University College, and All Souls), Georgian town houses, and older shop buildings, many of them timber-framed, with the tall spire of the University Church at its mid-point.

What made Oxford both unusual and special was that this patchwork of traditional shops and houses together with old university buildings – many of them with high walls, but with trees and ivy bringing colour into the honey-coloured stone (albeit stained with the soot of centuries) – was closely adjacent to abundant areas of green space. To the north of the historic city, the University Parks provided a mixture of spaces for sport and walking, and the dons' housing of North Oxford was gradually expanding into pleasant streets where the gardens of these new houses were full of trees. At the eastern end of the central university area, Magdalen College could boast an expansive deer park and a water meadow. Toward the west of the city was Port Meadow – 400 acres of grazing land and water meadow bordered by the Thames on one side, which had been common land since the Domesday Book recorded it as such in 1086. To the south of the older colleges in the centre of Oxford could be found Christ Church Meadow,

THE ORIGIN OF BOVADIUM

a large stretch of water meadow, bounded by the Thames (also referred to as the 'Isis' when it passes through Oxford) and the Cherwell rivers to its east and southern edges. Corpus Christi and Merton Colleges formed its northern boundary, together with the Botanic Gardens, which had been founded in 1621, with its original walls still largely intact, but with a recent addition of garden land leased to it by Christ Church.

Christ Church Meadow's origins go back to the twelfth century, the original land having been owned by the medieval religious institutions of St Frideswide's Priory and Oseney Abbey. The properties of St Frideswide were transferred to the new institution of Cardinal College in the 1520s, and then a few years later at the Reformation, Cardinal College became Christ Church, with the old Priory Church becoming the Cathedral of Oxford within the Church of England. The extensive land holdings of the Priory and the Abbey, including the Meadow land, were amalgamated and transferred to create Christ Church's extensive property portfolio. All through the middle ages and the upheaval of the sixteenth century the Meadow remained grazing land leased to local farmers, and water meadow. During the Civil War in the seventeenth century the natural borders created by the river and the Meadow were utilized by the Royalist army as part of the defensive line for the city during the Siege of Oxford, but this brief military episode did not spoil the essential bucolic charm of the Meadow. Elegiac lines in John Milton's *Il Penseroso* are reputed to have been inspired by the Meadow, and other writers, scholars and commentators have remarked on its special character noteworthy for its wildlife, botany (especially the famous snake's head fritillaries) and in particular its proximity to the buildings of the University and the city itself. For students, scholars and the citizens of Oxford to be able to walk around the Meadow (on well-established paths) was regarded throughout the period of Tolkien's residence in Oxford as a special amenity, one of the unique features of a city famous for its individual character.[1]

Oxford's beauty, formed by its unique combination of the adjacencies of superb architecture, unspoilt nature and antiquity meant that William Henry Fox Talbot, the inventor of photography, would choose Oxford as one of the first destinations for a

---

1   On the history of the Meadow see especially Judith Curthoys, *The Cardinal's College: Christ Church, Chapter and Verse* (London 2012), 22–35.

THE ORIGIN OF BOVADIUM

CHRIST CHURCH MEADOW - VIEW OF MERTON COLLEGE

photographic journey, and the subject matter for the first photographs to be included in a printed book, *The Pencil of Nature*, published in 1844. Oxford in the summer was, according to Talbot, 'the dwelling of the Genius of Repose'.[1]

Motopolis

The Oxford that Tolkien arrived at in 1911 had little in the way of manufacturing industry, the economy of the city being dominated by its role as a county

---

[1] William Henry Fox Talbot, *The Pencil of Nature* (London: Longman, 1844), text accompanying plate XVIII.

THE BOVADIUM FRAGMENTS

town. The city's industry was almost entirely focused on printing, with the University Press and other academic publishers driving the demand for paper (especially from the Wolvercote paper mill) and the print works in Jericho.[1] In the mid-nineteenth century the city had turned down an approach from Great Western Railways to host new workshops which would have employed over 1,500 workers. In contrast in 1911 the city was home to over 6,000 domestic servants, with fewer than 3% employed in engineering or allied trades.[2]

All of this would change dramatically thanks to the energy, drive and determination of one man, William R. Morris (later Lord Nuffield). Morris was born and raised in the city and began his commercial life through repairing bicycles; by the time Tolkien came to the city he had a workshop on Longwall Street where bicycles were repaired, and motor cars were sold, mostly to well-heeled undergraduates, through an agency operated by Morris.

---

1 Harry Carter, *Wolvercote Paper Mill: A Study in paper-making in Oxford* (Oxford: Oxford University Press, 1957).
2 Stephen Ward, Ossie Stuart, and Erik Swyngedouw, 'Cowley in the Oxford economy', in *The factory in the city: the story of the Cowley automobile workers in Oxford* eds. Teresa Hayter and David Harvey (London: Mansell, 1993), 67.

THE ORIGIN OF BOVADIUM

Around this time it dawned on Morris that there was a more lucrative opportunity than simply selling cars made by someone else. If he could manufacture his own vehicle, not only was there a ready market among the student body, he could make serious money not just in Oxford but across the whole nation. Thanks to significant start-up investment from a local grandee, the Earl of Macclesfield, Morris started to turn his idea into reality: the *Autocar* magazine in October 1912 reported that a new miniature light car had been put on the market by W.R.M. Motors of Longwall Street, Oxford, with a power rating of ten horsepower.[1] By 1913 Morris had purchased land from a former military training school in Cowley, to the east of the old city of Oxford, and had established a motor manufacturing plant. His first car would be called the 'Morris Oxford' and would become a firm favourite of the British public for decades to come. By the close of 1914 Morris was making 1,300 new cars a year, and by 1919 the company had grown in size and reputation, warranting a change of name: Morris Motors. Six years later the company was

---

1 Martin Adeney, *The Motor Makers: The turbulent history of Britain's car industry* (London, 1989), 79.

the largest motor manufacturer in the UK, and the Cowley car plant, as it moved towards genuine mass production, needed a constant stream of component parts. To supply this demand other industries began to establish factories in the city, one of which, the manufacture of pressed steel, was a joint financial venture between Morris and other investors. On the eve of the Second World War, the car industry in Oxford had grown from 200 employees in 1919 to over 10,000, spread across Morris Motors and the companies making component parts.[1] By 1965 this number had almost tripled to 28,000, and Morris Motors had become part of an industrial conglomerate called the Nuffield Corporation, which would swallow up many other automobile companies in the Midlands and even Australia.

Such spectacular growth would affect the city in numerous ways. To begin with it made Morris a wealthy man. By the time of the Second World War his personal wealth was turned to good use through philanthropic initiatives especially in the University's medical sciences (endowing individual professorships and eventually whole departments), and to various

---

1 Ward et al, 'Cowley in the Oxford economy', 71.

THE ORIGIN OF BOVADIUM

BATTALIONS OF MORRIS TRAVELLER CARS AT THE
COWLEY CAR PLANT

Oxford colleges, including establishing Nuffield College with entirely new buildings (which were modern but very much inspired by the local vernacular style) and a substantial endowment.[1]

The rise of Morris Motors would also alter the social structures of the city's population in profound

---

1   J.P.B. Dunbabin, 'Finance since 1914' in *History of the University of Oxford. Volume VIII: The Twentieth Century* ed. Brian Harrison (Oxford, 1994), 647–8.

ways. Oxford became the fastest growing city in the country between the wars, with a total population increasing from 67,290 in 1921 to 95,600 in 1939, an astonishing rise of 42%, driven in no small measure by the growth of the car industry. This profound demographic change created a rise in the demand for housing. Morris worked with the local authorities to encourage large-scale house building (such as the Bullingdon Fields estate) in Headington and Cowley, with the result that these suburbs grew so fast that they

WORKER AT THE COWLEY CAR PLANT

THE ORIGIN OF BOVADIUM

had to become administratively part of Oxford city. The pace would not slacken off after the war: between 1945 and 1973 more than 8,700 council houses were built, mostly to fill the demand of the motor industry's expanding workforce. Some of these new estates further expanded the topography of the city, such as at Blackbird Leys, where more than 23,000 dwellings were built on farmland from 1957 onwards.

A further demographic factor which the motor industry introduced to the city related to immigration. The insatiable demand for workers was met, in part, through encouraging migration from former Empire nations in South Asia and the Caribbean, introducing diversity into the city's ethnic mix, and bringing new occupants to the housing estates created with the motor industry in mind.

All of these changes built new communities, largely of working or lower middle class households in east Oxford, and with them community identities which would be contrasted for decades to come with the more genteel suburb of North Oxford, traditionally associated with the households of academics. These new urban (or perhaps suburban) identities, centred around Cowley, played into town planning discussions which would become an important factor in proposals for altering the flows of traffic, issues that would motivate Tolkien to write the *Bovadium Fragments*: 'it neither became the basis for a totally new Oxford, nor did it attain a full and independent identity separate from the old city.'[1]

The new industry, and the new identity for east Oxford that it created, brought the poet John Betjeman to identify three Oxfords: Christminster (the historic county town), University (for obvious reasons) and 'Motopolis'. 'To escapists, to arty people like the author of these pages,' he wrote, 'the internal combustion engine is, next to wireless, the most sinister modern invention . . . that its most successful manifestation in England should be at Oxford, of all places, passes belief.' Betjeman did, however, recognize the benefits that the industry brought to many: 'the most arty of us must hand it to William Morris the Second. He has given employment to thousands, and money to millions; he has provided a cheap means of transport to hundreds of thousands.'[2] To Betjeman these changes

---

1   Ward et al, 'Cowley in the Oxford economy', 83.
2   John Betjeman, *An Oxford University Chest* (London, 1938), 8. Betjeman's sardonic epithet reminds his readers that the industrialist was preceded by the influential artist, designer and writer of the same name.

THE ORIGIN OF BOVADIUM

were directly linked to the Morris factory: 'The fate of Oxford has been the fate of most country towns. But there is no doubt that the Morris Motor Works have helped to make the transformation so rapid and complete.' To add insult to injury, Betjeman added: 'Cambridge, for instance, comparatively unblessed by industrialism, still retains its character.'[1] Betjeman, who had been an undergraduate at Magdalen in the 1920s, was not alone among those regretting the rise of the motor car. Several articles appeared in the *Oxford Magazine* by angry dons in the 1930s and L.R. Phelps spoke for many when he wrote of 'the roar of traffic in the main streets is in painful contrast to the peace of the old days.'[2]

The rise of the city's industrial prowess, and the changes to its social structure and topography that were brought about by this growth, consequently had a profound impact on traffic in the city. This was especially felt in the old city, with its complex arrangement of small streets, alleys and vennels, which all combined to form the highly attractive centre, the

---

1 Betjeman, *Oxford University Chest*, 9.
2 Quoted in Richard Whiting, 'University and Locality' in *History of the University of Oxford. Volume VIII: The Twentieth Century* ed. Brian Harrison (Oxford, 1994), 569.

THE BOVADIUM FRAGMENTS

TRAFFIC CONGESTION AT CARFAX

atmosphere that Talbot had so lauded in the 1840s. The growth in traffic had started to become a major issue for the occupants of the colleges and houses in the old city as the new century dawned, associated particularly with the rise of the motor bus in 1913. In J.R.R. Tolkien's work *Roverandom*, which was conceived in 1925 while the family were briefly living in Leeds but not written up until 1927, the dog Rover (turned into a toy dog called Roverandom by a wizard)

THE ORIGIN OF BOVADIUM

has numerous extraordinary adventures (including visiting the dark side of the moon), but is assailed on his way home by the fumes and noise of heavy traffic.[1] The story gives us a sense at this early date of Tolkien's antipathy toward the motor car:

> Motor after motor racketed by, filled (Rover thought) with the same people, all making all speed (and all dust and all smell) to somewhere. "I don't believe half of them know where they are going, or why they are going there, or would know if they got there," grumbled Rover as he coughed and choked; and his feet got tired on the hard gloomy, black roads.[2]

Alfred Denis Godley (1856–1925), an Oxford Classics don at Magdalen College and a celebrated minor poet, was moved to write light comic, macaronic verses in 1914, entitled 'The Motor Bus', which were published in the *Oxford Magazine* and which complained of the impact of these new forms of public transport on the scholarly tenor of the High.

---

1 J.R.R. Tolkien, *Roverandom*; Catherine McIlwaine, *Tolkien: Maker of Middle-earth* (Oxford, 2018), 262.
2 J.R.R. Tolkien, *Roverandom* eds. Christina Scull and Wayne G. Hammond (London, 1998), 87.

THE BOVADIUM FRAGMENTS

> What is this that roareth thus?
> Can it be a Motor Bus?
> Yes, the smell and hideous hum
> Indicat Motorem Bum!

The poem continues along similar lines until ending with

> Domine defende nos
> Contra hos Motores Bos![1]

or: Lord defend us from these motor buses.

Tolkien may well have read this poem in the pages of the *Oxford Magazine* (a publication aimed at members of the University and written by dons, for the most part) while he was an undergraduate, but it remained a popular piece of verse in the city and the University long afterwards. A finely printed version of it, produced by the Sampson Press in 1927, can be found preserved in the Tolkien archive, filed along with the drafts of the *Bovadium Fragments*. It clearly struck a chord with Tolkien, chiming with his critique

---

1 MS. Tolkien B62/1 fols. 40r–v.

of the motor car expressed in the early versions of what would become *Roverandom*.

We can also get a sense of Tolkien's scathing view on modernity as it affected the built environment in Oxford from the drafts of the Andrew Lang Lecture that he was invited to give at the University of St Andrews on 8 March 1939, which would eventually be published as *On Fairy-Stories* in 1964. One passage (from an unpublished draft) in particular conveys his disgust for the march of modernity and the way in

UNDERGRADUATE LEAVING THE EXAMINATION
SCHOOLS ON THE HIGH STREET

THE BOVADIUM FRAGMENTS

which change was so warmly embraced by some of his colleagues in the University:

An Oxford don – incredible though it may sound – not long ago declared that he "welcomed" the proximity of mass-production robot factories, and the roar of self-obstructive mechanical traffic, because it brought the University into "contact with real life". He may have meant that the way men were living and working in the twentieth century was increasing in barbarity at an alarming rate, and that the kind of demonstration of this in the streets of Oxford might serve as a warning that it's not possible to preserve for long an oasis of sanity in a desert of unreason by mere fences, without actual offensive action (practical and intellectual). I fear he did not. In any case the expression "real life" in this context seems to fall short of academic standards. The notion that motor-cars are more "alive" than, say, centaurs or dragons is curious; that they are more real than, say, horses is pathetically absurd. How real, how startlingly alive is a factory chimney compared with an elm tree: poor obsolete thing, insubstantial dream of an escapist.[1]

---

1 MS. Tolkien 14, fol. 159r.

THE ORIGIN OF BOVADIUM

Oxford Replanned

Godley's humorous verse was based on a real-world problem, one of which the academic communities based in the colleges on the High Street were especially aware. Godley was a don at Magdalen College, and would only have to walk out of the college itself to experience the impact of the increased volumes of traffic crossing Magdalen Bridge, and travelling up and down the High Street, to and from the centre of Oxford and the shopping streets and markets; to this could be added the railway station which had been newly built on the west side of the city.

The historian Alan Bullock (writing in the early 1960s when he was both Master of St Catherine's College and Vice Chancellor) summed up the view of many about the city that Oxford was '. . . no longer the staid and sleepy university town of the nineteenth century, but a busy, crowded centre for an industrial population drawing its prosperity from the motor car factories at Cowley and spending lavishly in the chain stores which line Cornmarket.' The impact was felt most keenly, thought Bullock, on two of Oxford's most famous streets, The High and St Giles. Bullock

THE BOVADIUM FRAGMENTS

CARS ON BROAD STREET

regarded St Giles as having become an improvised car park, while the famous curve of the High 'is only to be appreciated on those rare occasions such as early Sunday morning when there is a pause in the incessant noisy flow of traffic.'[1]

A local historian, Lawrence Dale, came up with a plan in 1941 to rectify the growing problem. His plan was circulated as a small pamphlet called *Christ*

---

[1] Alan Bullock, 'Oxford: an introductory essay', in Cas Oorthuys, *Term in Oxford* (Oxford, 1963), 8.

THE ORIGIN OF BOVADIUM

Church Mall: A Diversion, which he published under the pseudonym 'Carfax'. In this little pamphlet Dale, then in his late fifties, summarized the problem in light, mocking tones:

> Have you ever been for a walk on Christ Church Meadow? No you have not; round it perhaps, by courtesy of the Dean, but not on it; the public are not allowed access to the Meadow.
> The Meadow must have belonged to the Priory of St Frideswide, and its successor, the House, from time immemorial . . . which is of course the argument for the cows and the grass and the railings remaining just as they always have been in saecula saeculorum.[1]

The author critically identified the chief issue:

> Now industry has raised its head in the east and commerce in the west (together with a railway station) and traffic of another kind possesses the street. Study is disturbed and the studious perturbed have to make undignified dashes under murderous wheels. The cobbles háve been replaced by tarmac . . .

---

1 [Lawrence Dale], *Christ Church Mall. A Diversion* (Oxford, 1941), 4–4.

THE BOVADIUM FRAGMENTS

In the meantime the cows continue to chew the cud in Christ Church Meadow.

He came up with a solution to the problem, one which brought modern ideas about town planning to accommodate new ways of living together in the city with the preservation of as much of the old ways as were feasible: a new road across the meadow:

> It is beyond question that the complaint that Oxford suffers from is arterio-sclerosis – the ancient arteries can no longer cope with the life that surges through them. To widen the arteries is to destroy that which we would preserve. Holywell for instance is threatened. A supplementary road running East and West is the only possible cure and across the Meadow the only possible route.

Three years later Dale came into the open and wrote a slightly longer piece under his own name, published by Faber, an important London publishing house. *Towards a Plan for Oxford City* was a much more serious intervention than his previous locally produced pamphlet, even though it retained its slightly mocking tones. 'I fly a kite,' he wrote: 'That

THE ORIGIN OF BOVADIUM

is how I got into disgrace. I flew a kite in Christ Church Meadow. It was September 1941. . . . It was quite a small kite, a little six-page pamphlet entitled *Christ Church Mall: A Diversion* in which I contrasted the fortunate circumstances of the cows in the Meadow, frisking in sixty-six acres of perfect peace, with the misfortunes of the Members of the University whose noble High Street was filled with an intolerable torrent of traffic.' To this extent he identified with the problems outlined in 1914 by Godley, and which were made much worse in the interwar period by the rise of the Cowley car plant and the growth of the suburban population there.

Dale's intention was to preserve the quiet atmosphere of the High, by untangling its centuries-old traffic routes:

> the famous High Street itself, the axis of the University, being the only connecting link between east and west; and the University, which had come to Oxford because of the seclusion it offered, found itself severed by a stream of traffic that entirely destroyed its scholarly quiet. Not only did the town sever the University, but the University cut the Town into two halves. . . . The immediate need of Oxford would

THE BOVADIUM FRAGMENTS

MAGDALEN COLLEGE TOWER FROM
NEW COLLEGE GARDENS

seem clearly to be the removal of this entanglement, to smooth out the traffic, to reintegrate both the town and the gown, so they both enjoyed what was necessary to them.[1]

His solution, however, would set in motion a series

---

1 Lawrence Dale, *Towards a Plan for Oxford City* (London, 1944), 23–26.

THE ORIGIN OF BOVADIUM

of political, social and academic disputes that would take three decades to be resolved and would divide those in both the city and the university, and would involve multiple reports, public inquiries, and even discussion in Cabinet.

The Sharp Plan

Oxford City witnessed tremendous growth in the first half of the twentieth century. In 1901 the city held 49,000 people in its administrative boundary, in 1921 the population had been just over 67,000, but by 1941 it had grown to over 108,000. The topographical constraints of the city meant that this extra body of people was accommodated by the building of suburbs in East Oxford (in close connection to the Cowley Car Works) and in Botley, Marston, and Linkside, where the growing middle classes could mingle: office workers, council and hospital staff, alongside the dons who were shunning the large, cold Victorian houses of North Oxford, which had been designed for an age where most middle-class households had servants. The middle classes of the 1950s and 60s were beginning to lead lives without these benefits.

THE BOVADIUM FRAGMENTS

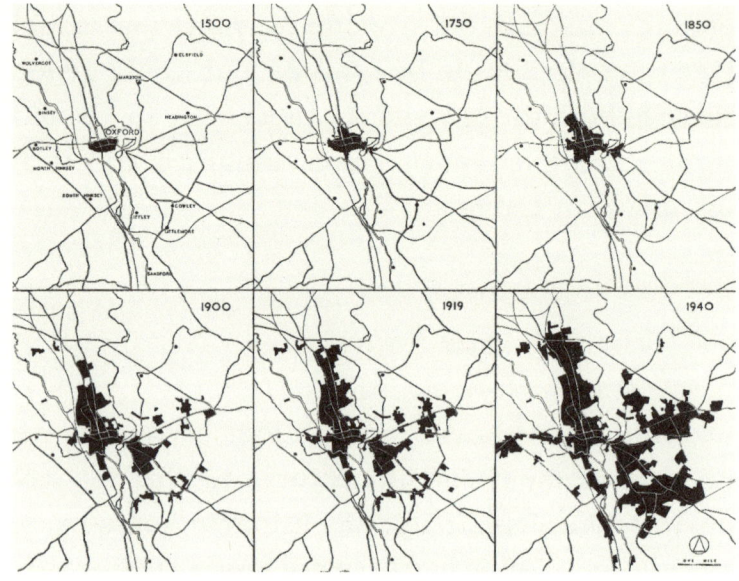

GROWTH OF OXFORD FROM SHARP'S PLAN

Many towns in 1950s Britain faced the future with optimism. The hardships of the inter-war years, and the ravages of the War itself were beginning to recede, and ahead lay a new society, one that was modern, forward-looking and embracing of technology. The social constraints which the War had helped to dislodge were further unsettled by the influx of new ideas about urban design and town planning pioneered by European architects and designers such as Le Corbusier, whose influence was felt on a generation of

THE ORIGIN OF BOVADIUM

British urban designers, architects and town planners such as Percy Johnson Marshall and Robert Matthew; around this time the concept of *townscape* as opposed to *landscape* came to influence this new discipline, with its post-war modernizing energy.[1] Lawrence Dale's ideas for how to solve the traffic and congestion crisis in Oxford were taken forward by the Oxford City Council's consultant, another of the major figures in post-war British town-planning, Thomas Sharp.

Sharp (1901–1978) was, by the time he was appointed by the City Council in May 1945, a celebrated town planner. Born in County Durham, he spent many years in the University's architecture department (then based at Newcastle), where he published a series of important books, including the influential *Town Planning* (1940). After a period based in London working for the Ministry of Works and Planning during the war, he then returned to town planning serving as a consultant on planning issues for several English towns including Exeter, Salisbury and Chichester. From 1945 onwards he was hired as a consultant by the Oxford City Council, working

---

1 Jerry Brotton and Nick Millea, *Talking Maps* (Oxford, 2019), 110.

to develop a coherent, comprehensive new plan for the city, dealing especially with the issues caused by traffic congestion. After three years of work, his plan (which he described as an 'outline') was published as *Oxford Replanned* in 1948.[1] Little did he realize the extent of public rancour that his plans would elicit over the coming three decades, although he must have been very conscious of them, as he had moved his consultancy and his home to North Oxford.[2]

Although *Oxford Replanned* was a report commissioned by the City Council, it circulated widely in published form as a book of over 200 pages, produced and distributed by the Architectural Press in London. The volume was printed to high standards, given that war-time rationing and other restrictions on paper and other elements of the publishing industry remained in force until 1949. The book was heavily illustrated with both historic engravings and newly-commissioned photography. Especially powerful were the many diagrams and maps, often in colour, which accompanied and explained Sharp's narrative. The book provides

---

1 Thomas Sharp, *Oxford Replanned* (London, 1948).
2 K.M. Stansfield, 'Thomas Wilfred Sharp (1901–1978)', Oxford Dictionary of National Biography. https://doi.org/10.1093/ref:odnb/31673.

a closely argued, and copiously illustrated, account of the historic growth of the townscape of Oxford, looking at broader social issues such as demographic change, and the growth of housing and industry. His study was combined with an analysis that showed carefully considered judgement on architectural and aesthetic grounds, examining issues concerning the city's built environment such as the optimal materials and textures that have been used to great effect in Oxford, as well as the play of light on the famous Oxford stone. More importantly, Sharp's work also brought forward proposals on how to develop the city into the future, with a focus on traffic planning.

Oxford Replanned contains no fewer than fifty-two 'main recommendations', some of which were broadly welcomed, but others, including limiting the City's population to 90,000, were always going to be unworkable. It was, however, the motor car that was central to his overall planning vision, including some very big ideas indeed, such as the wholesale relocation of the Oxford motor industry to the Midlands. The damage wrought by the motor car was the key element of his plan: 'A heavy concentration of traffic is threatening to break down the entire organisation of Oxford as a centre of civilised life,' he laid out in

THE BOVADIUM FRAGMENTS

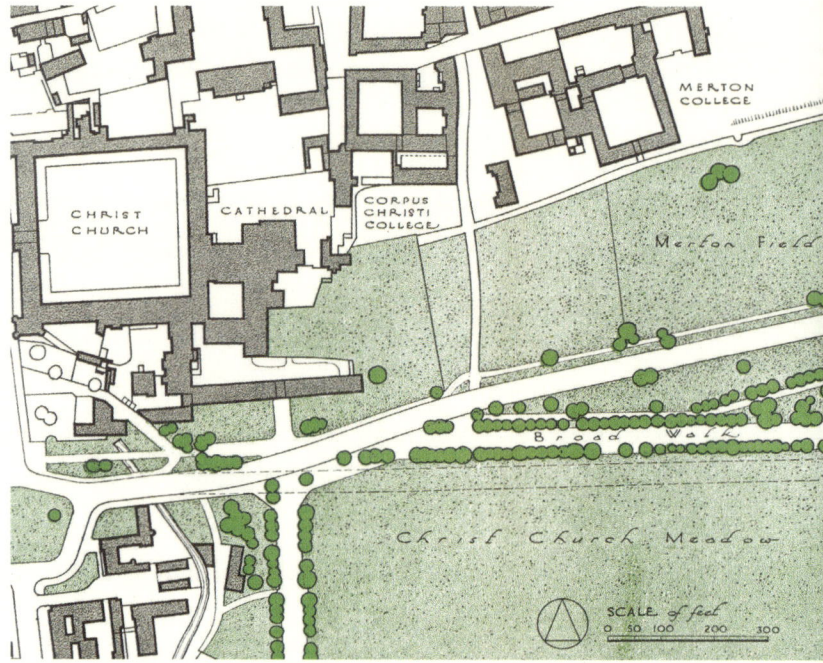

his plan. Tolkien would most likely have agreed with such a diagnosis. Sharp's focus on the position of the High within the topography of the City gave his ideas of solving the traffic problem a fulcrum from which all of the other elements would follow: 'it is the backbone of University life.'[1] Sharp's analysis moved logically to suggest a road across Christ Church Meadow, which he termed 'Merton Mall':

---

1   Sharp, *Oxford Replanned*, 19–21.

THE ORIGIN OF BOVADIUM

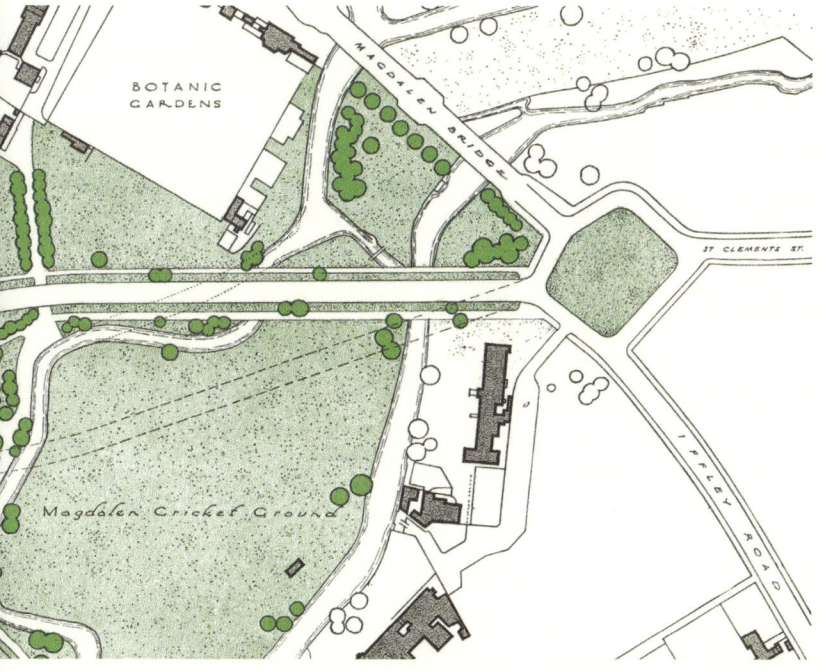

THE ROAD ACROSS CHRIST CHURCH MEADOW
– FROM SHARP'S PLAN

One of the main proposals in this plan is the road which it is proposed should run from the Plain, east of Magdalen Bridge, alongside the Broad Walk . . . to cross St Aldate's below Christ Church. . . . It has been called Merton Mall for purposes of identification. This proposal may cause bitter controversy. But it is the only possible means of relieving the mad traffic

THE BOVADIUM FRAGMENTS

> congestion in the High Street and of bringing some peace back into the old heart of the city. And it need not involve any destruction to the beauty of Christ Church Meadow, Broad Walk, or Merton Field. On the contrary, the new road could add to the beauty of those famous features of Oxford and would display it to far more people than ever see it now. . . . [1]

The plan for a road across Christ Church Meadow, as a means of alleviating traffic on the High, had already been established by Dale, and was now brought forward as the key to unlock the City's traffic problem by Sharp, in a much more thorough and considered way; but under his plan it also became part of a whole series of integrated schemes to reroute traffic through new roads. These included the completion of the outer ring road bypass (known today as the Oxford Ring Road) that was intended to operate in tandem with improvements to the arterial routes in and out of the city. These routes were themselves designed to operate with the new inner relief roads, of which the Meadow Road was the critical element (having been a part of the city's own dialogue dating back

---

1   Sharp, *Oxford Replanned*, 106.

to 1941 and Lawrence Dale's original notion). The plan would eventually include another proposed new road from the Marston Road across the University Parks, to emerge in St Giles, requiring the demolition of the Lamb and Flag pub (a much-loved hostelry). The Meadow Road was also linked to a new road through the city from St Aldate's (where the Meadow Road was intended to emerge), across to the Railway Station, helping to give the people of east Oxford easier access to the railway network.

The northern Inner Relief Road (as it was sometimes called) through the University Parks would become, for a time, even more controversial than

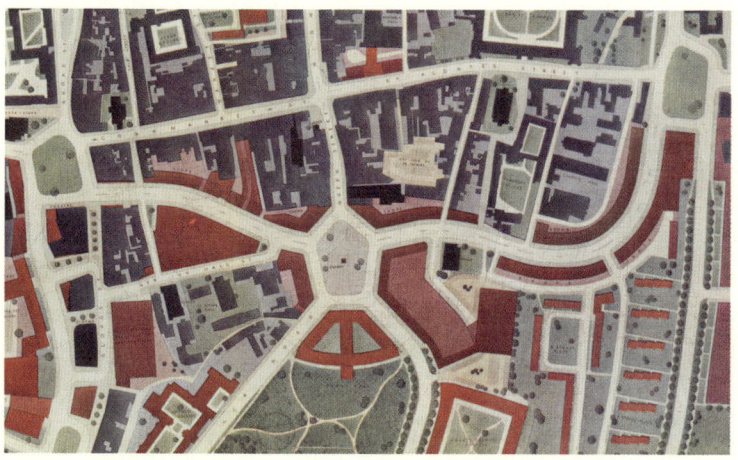

SHARP'S PROPOSED NEW ROAD LAYOUTS

the Meadow Road plan. Its proximity to the science department in the growing science area of the University based either side of South Parks Road produced outraged comments from that part of the Oxford academic community, with assertions being made that many of the scientists would leave the University if the plans for the road went ahead.

Sharp's plans were initially given a broad welcome. The report's publication was accompanied by a public exhibition of the proposals. Sharp issued his ideas to the city and to the world with a challenge: 'it is now for the citizens of Oxford, and for all those who love the city and have its future at heart, to decide what shall be done. The city is their charge. Theirs is the responsibility for the future.'[1] A reviewer in *Planning Outlook* felt that 'in analysing the urban scene in language understandable by the citizen Mr. Sharp has done much to widen the layman's appreciation of old Oxford; Oxford the work of art and national heritage.'[2] The young scholar J.N.L. Myres, who would later become Bodley's Librarian, reviewing the book in *Oxoniensia* regarded it as 'lively, intelligent,

---

1 Cited in Brotton and Millea, *Talking Maps*, 111.
2 T.F.L., 'Co-operative communities', *Planning Outlook Series*, 1 (1948), 50–53.

original, far-sighted, and extremely provocative'; he went on to doubt 'whether any book about Oxford has ever stimulated so many people to write and think so much about the city.' He also pointed out that the vast majority of comment had focused on just a few of the more controversial proposals, including 'Merton Mall' and the 'plan for a new road along the northern margin of the Parks', and that much else in the book had been overlooked. He confessed, however, that these were 'matters of first importance for Oxford's future', and therefore deserved the attention they had received.[1] On 4 May 1947 at a debate in the Oxford Union, the motion was carried that 'this House welcomes Dr Sharp's proposals for the replanning of Oxford.'[2]

From Merton Mall to Sandys Mall

The Sharp plans, discussed and debated as they were, took a major step forward thanks to the passing of the Town and Country Planning Act in 1947. This

---

1   J.N.L. Myres, 'Oxford Replanned', *Oxoniensia*, 13 (1948), 89–93.
2   Roland Newman, *The Road and Christ Church Meadow* (Minster Lovell, 1988), 10.

THE BOVADIUM FRAGMENTS

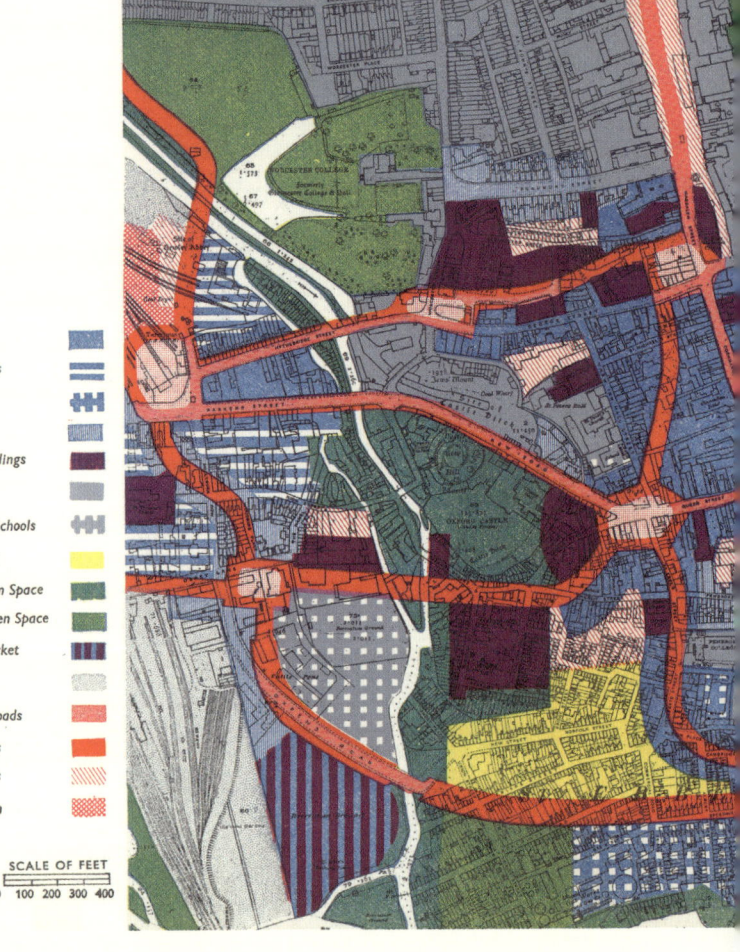

THE ORIGIN OF BOVADIUM

PROPOSALS FOR MERTON MALL AND OTHER ROADS

required local authorities to submit a Development Plan to the Minister within three years. Given the state of the nation after the war, this was a tall order, and the Oxford City response was not submitted until 1953. This did not originally include the main Sharp proposals relating to the inner relief roads. The Minister at the time, Duncan Sandys, asked for a resubmission so that measures to relieve the city centre from excessive traffic could be included. Sandys, like many in the Conservative administration at the time, was Oxford educated, having been an undergraduate at Magdalen College, and even though he graduated in 1929, the traffic congestion on the High was severe enough by then to have left its mark on the budding politician.

On 27 August 1955 the great historian Hugh Trevor-Roper, then a don at Christ Church, wrote to his friend the art historian Bernard Berenson, giving him news from Oxford. The Meadow Road was the major news, and Trevor-Roper focused his ire on the Warden of New College, A.H. Smith, the Vice Chancellor at the time, who he felt had badly handled the University's management of the issue. 'For the British Motorist, having invested large sums of money in his motor car naturally expects some return on his investment . . . he is therefore mortified to discover that, when thrusting his way through Oxford, he is continually held-up by traffic blocks and has to witness armies of low-class pedestrians sweeping past at 3 miles per hour.' Trevor-Roper continued that the motorist cried: 'away . . . with these obstructions, these University buildings which impede the march of petrol and progress! Let us have a huge turnpike road that ignores such obstacles!' In the midst of these cries, so Trevor-Roper suggested, the Vice Chancellor had whispered the solution: 'a Road through the Meadow and a Grass-Grown High Street'.[1]

Vice Chancellor Smith's support for the plans for an inner relief road gradually became more public, and *The Times* of 19 May 1955 reported a meeting of the Oxford Society (a civic organization) where he spoke in favour of plans to remove traffic from the city centre.[2] As the Vice Chancellor's support of the scheme became more widely known, so the opposition within the University began to take shape. One of the leaders was Robert Blake, a noted historian

---

1 *Letters from Oxford: Hugh Trevor-Roper to Bernard Berenson* ed. Richard Davenport-Hines (London, 2006), 179.
2 Newman, *The Road and Christ Church Meadow*, 12.

at Christ Church, who wrote a response in *The Times* a few weeks later, saying that Christ Church would oppose the road 'by every legitimate means'. The staunch opposition of Christ Church brought criticism from many in the University who were not directly affected by the schemes. Maurice Bowra, the Warden of Wadham College, spoke for many when he remarked in a letter to a friend that 'we must be in a position to negotiate and not rely on simply saying "no".'[1]

The temperature surrounding the planning debate was getting hotter, and the thermometer would be dramatically raised in September 1956 when Sandys wrote to the City Council rejecting various proposed schemes and forcing the authorities to focus on the relief of traffic in the centre of the city, making it clear that in discussion with the Minister for Transport he had agreed that the High Street should cease to be used for through traffic. The Meadow Road was, in the Minister's opinion, 'the only feasible solution' to Oxford's traffic problem. The proposed road became known, for a while, as 'Sandys Mall'.

Oxford was full of intrigue concerning the issue

---

1   Cited in Whiting, 'University and locality', 573.

THE ORIGIN OF BOVADIUM

as the 1950s progressed. Camps began to be formed along clear-cut lines (especially in the University, where lines were drawn between the High Street colleges on the one side and the Meadow colleges on the other). The social and academic networks of Oxford dons were brought to bear on the warfare surrounding the plans. Trevor-Roper's report to Berenson described intense lobbying: 'Of course as you can imagine, the Opposition is organizing furiously. Ministers are being lobbied in country houses, and the fact that half the House of Lords were at Christ Church is not being left unexploited by my more active colleagues.'[1] The undergraduate newspaper the *Cherwell* reported in October 1955 that the college community was split with fifteen opposed to the plans and ten in favour.[2] Tolkien's views on the specifics of the plan are not known, but on the general issue of the pressure of traffic on the character of the city at this time they were clear: 'the spirit of Isengard, if not of Mordor, is of course always cropping up,' he wrote to Michael Straight in 1956, 'the present

---

1 Davenport-Hines, *Letters from Oxford*, 180.
2 William Whyte, 'Lost causeways: Oxford, experts and the motor age' in *Resplendent adventures with Britannia: personalities, politics and culture in Britain* ed. William Roger Louis (London, 2015), 294.

design of destroying Oxford in order to accommodate motor-cars is a case.'[1]

One of the reasons why the Meadow Road plan aroused so much discussion and debate was that, although the core problem was generally agreed upon, Sharp's proposed solution polarized opinion both in Oxford and beyond. One senior member of Christ Church, John Lowe, was brave enough to go out on his own and publish a flysheet in the *Oxford Magazine* in favour of the Meadow plan. These printed sheets laid out positions ahead of debates in congregation: 'Do you want to leave things substantially as they now are, with the High Street turned into a second Cornmarket and lorries and buses pouring in an increasing flood along Holywell and Catte Street,' his statement argued, 'or do you wish to accept this new plan that will give us a unified University to which the peace and beauty of the past will be restored? We have been talking for years about saving the University; – if you reject this plan it will be clear that these were empty words, and that you prefer to save a Meadow.'[2]

The Master of University College (situated directly

---

1   *The Letters of J.R.R. Tolkien* eds. Humphrey Carpenter and Christopher Tolkien (London, 2023), 340.
2   MS. Eng.c.3028 Papers of A.L. Goodhart, fol. 43r.

THE ORIGIN OF BOVADIUM

TRAFFIC ON THE HIGH STREET

on the High), Goodhart, spoke in a Congregation debate on the traffic planning issue, pitting the pressures faced by those in the colleges on the High against the more bucolic situation of Merton and Christ Church: 'It is not usually realized that for those living along the High the greatest objection to the use of this street by the buses and heavy lorries is the continual noise and vibration. . . . When the traffic is removed it will be possible again to enjoy life in comparative calm in the rooms facing the High. . . . The road across the Meadows will have a disadvantageous effect on Christ Church and on Merton. In the case of Christ Church the road will be at the worst within 150 feet of the Meadow buildings. . . . [I]n the case of Merton the new road will be separated from the College by the Merton playing fields, and it will therefore be more than 500 feet away.'[1]

The Fight Back

From this point on a concerted campaign to oppose the plans emerged, and Robert Blake was able to get his college to make explicit their corporate opposition to the plan, as part of developing a single University position for a public inquiry called by the Council. They published a statement in the *Oxford Mail* on 29 September 1956 stating of the Meadow Road plan that: 'It is one of the greatest acts of vandalism that could have been perpetrated. We are astounded that the Minister should have the effrontery to put forward

---

1 MS. Eng.c.3028 Papers of A.L. Goodhart, fols. 21r–22r.

THE ORIGIN OF BOVADIUM

a proposal of this nature in so arbitrary a fashion.' Words were followed with action from the college, which issued a writ against the Minister challenging his actions to direct the City Council on procedural grounds.

The public inquiry of 1956 resulted in one of Sharp's ideas, that of the northern relief road through the University parks being dropped, and the Meadow Road firmly established as the Council's and the Minister's preferred option: 'the loss of quiet at the northern end of the Meadow will be greatly outweighed by the gain of peace and dignity in the heart of the University.'[1] A traffic survey reported in 1959, confirming the view that the Meadow Road was the only viable solution to Oxford's traffic problem.

With the Council's position being backed by the Ministry, the turn of the decade saw the fight back against the Meadow Road become stronger, emboldened by a public inquiry which was conceded to by the Government in a debate in the House of Lords, with the opposition being led by Lord Beaverbrook. The University's position had shifted considerably

---
1 Newman, *The Road and Christ Church Meadow*, 14.

since the middle of the previous decade, but it still equivocated on the outright opposition to the Meadow Road plan. The plan was still on the table, but only if it could be proven that there was no viable alternative. At a hearing for the public inquiry at the Town Hall in December 1960, the submission from the Provost and Fellows of Worcester College summed up the mood of many in the University:

> The College considers that relief should be given to the central area by the completion of the outer bypasses, the Cowley centre, new parking places, intermediate roads, and appropriate restrictions on the use of motor vehicles; and that, even if its views on the protection of the central area are rejected, no decision should be made to construct any inner relief road unless and until the need for doing so has been established beyond doubt after observing the effects of such measures.[1]

The intensity of the public debate on the issue ratcheted up through the decade. The pages of both national and local newspapers were full of articles in

---

1   MS. Eng.c.3028 Papers of A.L. Goodhart, fol. 12r.

THE ORIGIN OF BOVADIUM

1960, as were their letters pages. Even that beloved national institution, Alistair Cooke's 'Letter from America' on BBC Radio 4, devoted time to covering the issue. Rather remarkably Cooke cited the notorious New York City developer Robert Moses (at this point his ruthless working methods were yet to be exposed in Robert Caro's famous study of him, *The Power Broker*) in opposition to the plan:

> Don't monkey with your parks because they seem to offer precious space for more cars. If you put divided highways in the middle of a city and trim your parks to provide for them, then all you do is attract more and more traffic to the centre of the city.[1]

It was at this point in the debate that Tolkien was moved to write *The Bovadium Fragments*. Tolkien's perspective had been created through his own lived experience of the city. He had been an undergraduate at Exeter College in the college's buildings on Turl Street, right in the centre of the old city, with his final year being spent in rooms in a Georgian building on St John Street. After the war, while working on

---

1 Broadcast on 21 May 1961.

THE BOVADIUM FRAGMENTS

STUDYING IN THE DUKE HUMFREY'S LIBRARY
IN THE BODLEIAN

the staff of the *New English Dictionary* (based in the glorious late seventeenth-century building of the Old Ashmolean on Broad Street) he had returned to live on St John Street; although architecturally different to his college rooms, his early Oxford experience was all spent in the centre of the city. The clogging up of these streets with traffic (with the sound and air pollution that went with it), and the proposed threat

THE ORIGIN OF BOVADIUM

to the ancient bucolic treasure of Christ Church Meadow, must have seemed deeply threatening to Tolkien.

He had continued to regret the ever-growing dominance of the motor car in Oxford. In a letter to Joan Tolkien in 1961 he remarked that 'Oxford continues to suffer from the ravages of the machine-worshippers.' His nostalgia brought him to remember Oxford as 'a little old university town nestling in the country – and it had about 55,000 inhabitants. It now has nearly 100,000 *more,* sprawls in every direction, and is jammed with noise and smell . . . '.[1]

In October 1960, having finished a draft of *The Bovadium Fragments,* Tolkien wrote to Rayner Unwin, whose family publishing house George Allen and Unwin had published his Middle-earth works since *The Hobbit* was first issued in 1937. Tolkien asked Unwin for the name of whoever was editing the weekly literary magazine, *Time and Tide,* which had a wide circulation and had a broadly Christian editorial theme, and published work by fellow Inklings C.S. Lewis and Charles Williams. Indeed, the first review of *The Lord of the Rings* had appeared in the magazine,

---

1 Carpenter & Tolkien, *Letters,* 438.

THE BOVADIUM FRAGMENTS

written by Lewis.[1] Whether the typescript was ever sent to the magazine is not known. (By 1968 he was referring to the work as 'The End of Bovadium', without any intention of publishing it.)[2]

As Tolkien was writing up *The Bovadium Fragments* and still at that time contemplating publishing the work, the City Council's proposals for the Meadow Road were coming to a critical point. The public inquiry eventually concluded that traffic relief would only be possible with a Meadow Road, and in 1962 the then Minister for Housing and Local Government, Dr Charles Hill, upheld its findings. A firm of London architects, Jellicoe and Coleridge, were hired to develop more detailed plans, accepting in principle the line of the road across the Meadow that the Minister had approved. Their plans had to be conscious of the public mood, their preface stating that: 'Because it is tranquil, the meadow at present is complimentary to the city. The primary endeavour of this design has been to retain this tranquility

---

1 Humphrey Carpenter, *J.R.R. Tolkien: A Biography* (London, 1977), 219.
2 *The J.R.R. Tolkien Companion and Guide: Chronology* eds. Christina Scull and Wayne G Hammond, Revised and expanded edition (London, 2017), 774.

THE ORIGIN OF BOVADIUM

and therefore to suppress the road and its attendant architecture.'

The reaction in Oxford was predictably forthright: the Treasurer of Christ Church reported that the college's view was that the outcome was 'disastrous for the planning of Oxford' and the Warden of Merton felt it was 'aesthetically barbarous'.[1]

Another public inquiry would soon follow, in order to settle the debate that continued to rage in both Oxford and in London. The University appointed a planning counsel to represent them in the 1965 inquiry. A new figure appeared on the scene who would be as influential in the debate as Thomas Sharp himself. Professor Colin Buchanan (1907–2001) was a distinguished town planner specializing in transport, having worked at the Ministry of Transport in the 1930s, and served with the Royal Engineers in North Africa during the war. In 1946 he joined the newly created Ministry of Town and Country Planning. In his spare time Buchanan published *Mixed Blessing: the Motor in Britain* which brought him to the attention of Ernest Marples, Minister for Transport, who persuaded Buchanan to move to his Ministry.

---

1   Newman, *The Road and Christ Church Meadow*, 21.

THE BOVADIUM FRAGMENTS

From his base in the Ministry, Buchanan led a team that in 1963 produced a report entitled *Traffic in Towns*, which introduced the idea of minimum standards for noise, pollution and other environmental factors relating to traffic in areas of high population. The report was hugely influential, and on the back of its success Buchanan left the civil service, moving to Imperial College London as their first Professor of Transport, which he held whilst also forming his own consultancy, Colin Buchanan and Partners. It was from his academic position that Buchanan was asked to produce a report as part of the University's evidence submitted to the 1965 public inquiry.[1]

The Standing Counsel for the University, Sir Edward Milner Holland, and Professor Buchanan decided that the case for the city could best be demolished by demonstrating at the inquiry the depth of opposition. In addition to the performative aspects of this opposition Buchanan submitted a proof of over forty pages with a detailed analysis of the question of the Meadow Road, which very effectively dismantled the argument. His view was summarized:

---

1 Peter Hall, 'Sir Colin Douglas Buchanan (1907–2001)', *Oxford Dictionary of National Biography*, https://doi.org/10.1093/ref:odnb/76552.

THE ORIGIN OF BOVADIUM

In my opinion, as a town planner of wide experience, the Meadow in its present form and in its entirety constitutes an asset to Oxford of the most remarkable kind. I doubt whether there is another city in the world, still less a city which is a great seat of learning, which provides almost in its centre a comparable scene of pastoral remoteness and simplicity, isolated from Motor traffic.

The conclusion was obvious, he felt: 'No reasonable person could wish to see a road built across Christ Church Meadow. . . . The Minister should order a fresh comprehensive approach.'[1]

Dick Williamson, then a junior lawyer working at the Oxford firm of solicitors Morrell, Peel, and Gamlen that acted for the University (and who would act on behalf of J.R.R. Tolkien and later the Tolkien Estate and Trust), was instructed to round up submissions from a variety of worthies from Town (city) as well as Gown (university). The people he got agreement from included Alan Bullock (then both Principal of St Catherine's College and Vice Chancellor), Dunstan

---

1 Oxford University Archives UR6/CQ/1B (sub), file 4, Proofs of Evidence, 1965. Proof of Evidence by Professor C.D. Buchanan.

THE BOVADIUM FRAGMENTS

Skilbeck (Principal of Wye College in Kent, who was called to cover the agricultural value of the Meadow), and the Heads of Worcester, Trinity, Lincoln, St John's, Lady Margaret Hall and Somerville colleges. The local photographer Raymond Stanton King, Sir Basil Blackwell, Tom Driberg (a local MP and Christ Church man) and Osbert Lancaster, the cartoonist, read out their proof of evidence and were available for cross-examination, but the Counsel for the City declined to cross-examine any of the University's witnesses as they were all speaking in favour of the Meadow as a place of beauty, a fact not disputed by the City. There was, however, one exception in Mrs Christian Hardie who was called as 'an Oxford Housewife'. Harold Marnham, Junior Counsel for the City, took the opportunity to cross-examine her, claiming that as the wife of an Oxford don she was very much part of the 'Gown'. She responded robustly saying that the Junior Counsel for the City seemed to have little idea of what happens in Oxford, adding that whether this was personal ignorance or lack of instruction, she did not know.[1]

---

1 I owe this account to the late Dick Williamson, who kindly shared his notes with me.

THE ORIGIN OF BOVADIUM

The Battle Won

The debate over the Meadow Road in the middle of the 1960s took a decisive turn when it became clear to those opposing the road that the city would have to cease appeasing the motorist. Buchanan made this explicit in his evidence: 'the idea of being tougher with the motorist has revolutionized the position.'[1] By the end of the public inquiry, Buchanan's evidence, and the organized presentation of other expert witnesses from both within the university (Gown) and from the city (Town) saw the proposal for the Meadow Road change to one which ran well to the south of Sharp's proposed route. This road (now called Donnington Bridge Road) would run from the southern end of the Iffley Road and run across the river to the Abingdon Road's southerly end, enabling the east-west link up that Dale and Sharp had correctly identified, but without encroaching on Christ Church Meadow itself. The Sharp plans had also suggested redevelopment of the poor-quality housing at St Ebbe's. This too would eventually come to pass, together with a

---

1 Whiting, 'University and locality', 573.

new road from St Aldate's to the train station (Oxpens Road), which were other badly needed elements of improvement to the city, but which were held up for decades while the debate over the Meadow Road continued to rage. For a while the Meadow plan would still be tentatively pushed forward, but the Secretary of State for the Environment in 1971, Peter Walker, eventually put an end to the discussion, debate and rancour over the Meadow Road once and for all. The deciding factor for him was 'the unique and irreplaceable character of Christ Church Meadow itself, which is of importance far beyond the boundaries of the University or City.'[1]

Conclusion

The Meadow Road was an extraordinary episode in the history of Oxford, but also in the history of town planning, *because* it related to Oxford, with its combination of Town and Gown, and where the University had educated many of the men who would make key decisions in Government. The question was

---

1   Newman, *The Road and Christ Church Meadow*, 27.

THE ORIGIN OF BOVADIUM

even discussed in Cabinet, so Lord (David) Eccles reported in a debate in the House of Lords in 1963:

> the voices were pitched high; tempers were ruffled; passions were out in full force. The Balliol and New College men were on one side, the Magdalen and Christ Church men were on the other, while the Cambridge men looked down their noses in smug silence. No page of fiction, no ugly scene from the novels of Sir Charles Snow, could equal that abortive struggle.[1]

'Oxford is not a Museum,' wrote Alan Bullock in 1963, 'and no one who lives and works in it supposes it can remain a great university without facing far-reaching changes.'

In the midst of the public debate over the plans, which it would have been hard to be unaware of in Oxford in the 1950s and 1960s, J.R.R. Tolkien wrote *The Bovadium Fragments*. Although satirical, it was good humoured and moderate in tone, though the message is clear – the role of planners in changing the environment in which people lived in order to

---

1 Hansard, *House of Lords Debates*, vol. 563, 12 December 1963, col. 1347.

THE BOVADIUM FRAGMENTS

work and live, and in giving priority to the motor car, was both dangerous and negative. The changes that Bullock alluded to were not welcomed by Tolkien, and *The Bovadium Fragments* was his contribution to the debate.

Tolkien's views on the motor car have already been discussed, but the specifics of the impact of the motor car and the motor industry must be seen in the broader context of Tolkien's own sensibilities

CAR TRANSPORTER OUTSIDE BALLIOL COLLEGE

THE ORIGIN OF BOVADIUM

regarding modern life. From the perspective of the twenty-first century we might think of *The Bovadium Fragments* as a contribution to environmental literature, writing that is critical of man-made intrusions into the natural environment. Many doctoral theses, journal articles and entire books have been written in recent years on Tolkien's imaginative writing and his concern for nature and the environment.

To any reader of Tolkien's creative writing, the focus of *The Bovadium Fragments* comes as no surprise. His love of the natural environment is expressed throughout his Middle-earth work, both in the text and his own illustrations, and in a letter to Rhona Beare in 1958 he remarked that 'I visualize with great clarity and detail scenery and "natural" objects.'[1] Trees were of particular importance for Tolkien, as he wrote to Jane Neave in 1962: 'Every tree has its enemy, few have an advocate,' and in 1972 he wrote in the *Daily Telegraph* that 'in all my works I take the part of trees as against all their enemies.'[2]

Tolkien had a deep love for nature, but he also had a deep love for rural life, especially the older

---

1   Carpenter & Tolkien, *Letters*, 400.
2   Carpenter & Tolkien, *Letters*, 453, 588–9.

pre-industrial way of life in which man lived and worked in the countryside. His childhood visits to rural Worcestershire in the early years of the twentieth century gave him the opportunity to experience at first hand a way of life that was fast disappearing, and this would stay with him: 'Any corner of that county ... is in an indefinable way "home" to me, as no other part of the world is.'[1] This love of English rural life, imbued in Tolkien from such an early age, would find its way into his creative writing, especially as expressed in the Shire, the home of the Hobbits. The penultimate chapter of *The Lord of the Rings* sees the triumphant but exhausted Hobbits return at last to their beloved Shire, Frodo and Sam's 'own country', the place 'that they cared about ... more than any other place in the world.' Here, at the end of their epic adventures, where they had hoped to return to their old life, unchanged, they received instead a 'really painful shock' seeing the traditional homes deserted or burned down, and what was worse, 'looking with dismay up the road towards Bag End they saw a tall chimney of brick in the distance. It was pouring out

---

1 Quoted in Humphrey Carpenter, *J.R.R. Tolkien: A Biography* (London, 1977), 19.

black smoke into the evening air.'[1] These devastating changes were accompanied by authoritarian rule that threatened not just the environment to which the Hobbits had hoped to return, but the social order. Eventually the Hobbits would defeat the 'ruffians' (led by Saruman) but as they returned to Bag End:

> the great chimney rose up before them; and as they drew near the old village across the Water, through rows of new mean houses along each side of the road, they saw the new mill in all its frowning and dirty ugliness: a great brick building straddling the stream, which it fouled with a steaming and stinking overflow. All along the Bywater Road every tree had been felled.[2]

Such a moving and powerful evocation stands in a line begun earlier by writers such as William Morris and Gerard Manley Hopkins, who shared a love of nature with a love of Oxford.

Tolkien was especially familiar with Hopkins's writings, and must have known of his famous poem 'Binsey Poplars', which has also come to be

---

[1] J.R.R. Tolkien, *The Lord of the Rings. Part III: The Return of the King* (London, 1955), 283.
[2] J.R.R. Tolkien, *Return of the King*, 296.

considered a classic work of environmental literature. In it Hopkins lamented the felling of trees along the Thames path at Binsey, a tiny hamlet within easy walking distance of central Oxford:

> My aspens dear, whose airy cages quelled,
> Quelled or quenched in leaves the leaping sun,
> All felled, felled, are all felled;
> Of a fresh and following folded rank
> Not spared, not one
> That dandled a sandalled
> Shadow that swam or sank
> On meadow and river and wind-wandering
> weed-winding bank.[1]

The melancholy that 'Binsey Poplars' is steeped in also pervades the end of *The Lord of Rings* with the sense of time coming to reckon with the old established ways of living. J.R.R. Tolkien was not an active combatant in the war against modernity and the motor car in Oxford, or even the battle against the Meadow Road, but *The Bovadium Fragments* suggests

---

1 Gerard Manley Hopkins, *Poems* 3rd edition eds. Robert Bridges and W.H. Gardner (Oxford, 1948), 83.

THE ORIGIN OF BOVADIUM

ANCIENT AND MODERN

that he was prepared, in his own way, to play his part. As Saruman's forces are vanquished in the Shire, Sam Gamgee exclaimed: 'And that's the end of that,' and his completed sentence could have been written as a comment on the saga of the Meadow Road: 'A nasty end, and I wish I needn't have seen it; but it's a good riddance.'[1]

RICHARD OVENDEN OBE

---

1 Tolkien, *Return of the King*, 300.

ACKNOWLEDGEMENTS

I would like to thank many of my colleagues in Oxford who gave valuable help during the research for this piece: Judith Curthoys, Julia Walworth, William Whyte, Dick Williamson, and within the Bodleian, Nick Millea, Faye MacLeod, the staff of the Special Collections Reading Rooms, and especially Catherine McIlwaine, Tolkien Archivist. Huge thanks to Martin Parr for introducing me to the photography of Cas Oortuhys in Oxford. Finally, I would like to express my profound thanks to Baillie and Christopher Tolkien. On one of my visits to stay with them, Christopher told me about the Bovadium Fragments, and we had a long discussion about them and their origin. It was his idea for us to collaborate on the book. I miss his warmth, his sense of humour, and his deep knowledge, but give thanks for having known him.

R.O.